CONFESSIONS OF A
GEEK BARD

CONFESSIONS OF A
GEEK BARD

MIKEY MASON

Charlotte, NC

FALSTAFF
BOOKS
WWW.FALSTAFFBOOKS.COM

For Tran, Thorin, Toho, Hiram, and all the other people I never was, but was all along.

HOW WE GOT HERE...

I was at ConCarolinas in Charlotte, NC in June of 2021, taking a walk with my wife, Jody, when we bumped into John Hartness. I was pretty sure they'd met, at least informally, at some point but made sure to give a proper introduction anyway. I'd known John from his *Authors & Dragons* podcast and panels, and from conventions and events, and I knew he was an author and publisher at Falstaff Books. I began to joke with John, as I always tend to when I'm around folks who make their livings with words, about someday putting my creative writing degree to use for something other than songs, when John gave me a flat look and said, "I'll offer you a contract this weekend, right here at this convention, to write a book of song lyrics and stories about the songs."

He was serious, and I knew it. But a book is a scary proposition, and a contractual agreement to complete one even more so, at least to me. I was fairly noncommittal, but I admit, he had my curiosity piqued. I'd had a short story published before, in a Kickstarted anthology, but this—this was different. This wasn't a crowdfunded effort or a vanity press, and there's something ominous about the words *contractually obligated*. But John is a charismatic man, and I liked the idea. Before a week was out, I'd discussed the book with him and signed a contract. Just like that, I was under contract to be a published author, contractually obligated to write the book you're holding now.

So... What kind of a book is it, exactly? It's not exactly a memoir, though certainly the stories have been drawn from my memory. It's not just a collection of lyrics from my songs and parodies, though many are included here. It's not exactly album liner notes or a behind the scenes deep-dive into songwriting, although there are undeniable aspects of that, as well. It's more of a verbal patchwork quilt pieced together out of all those things, as well as my own commentary and opinions (which are, fair warning, subject to change without notice). I'll try and make the factual bits as factual as possible, but any opinions stated herein are simply the codified thoughts I had at the time of writing, and I reserve the right to grow and change and become a different (hopefully better) person.

The songs, and therefore the accompanying stories, are presented in the order that makes the most sense to me, from personal, historical, and storytelling perspectives. Sometimes I defer to when a song was written, sometimes I defer to when it was published on an album or as a single. Sometimes I defer to a specific version of a song, if more than one version was published. There were internal methods to my particular madness, as unexplained or unexplainable as they might be, and I hope they don't detract from the overall work.

Finally, there are many stories (not to mention very important people) who didn't make it into this book. I'd apologize for that, except that it might not be entirely a good thing to be included in the book, I guess. There are many folks I love whose names do not grace these pages. This wasn't a book about all of my favorite people, or anything of the sort. It's a collection of stories and song lyrics, and maybe even just a first volume (though let's not get carried away).

I've done my best to make it as entertaining and engaging as possible. These songs are children of mine, the memories are personal ones. The stories are, sometimes, not ones I share often. This book holds pieces of my life, rearranged for your entertainment. If you don't like it, by all means, don't feel like you have to. Be honest. But also be kind. Because if you can be anything in the world, you should at least be kind.

THE HALFLING SONG

[LYRICS REDACTED]

I t seems a bit like cheating to me to begin a book of song lyrics and stories with a song whose lyrics I fully have no intention of sharing with you, but here we are. I feel like this story is the place to start because it's the beginning, the truest beginning I can find when I search the archives of my memories. It is a story of portent, even if it was portent missed at the time. That's okay. We humans miss a lot of things because we're not paying as much attention to what's happening when it happens as we are to what we think we want to happen.

As you might have expected, what with this being written by me, and me being who I am, this is a gaming story. What you will likely find equally unsurprising is that it all began with a song: a silly, improvised, spur-of-the-moment song that I swear before all that is holy I still remember word for word, note for note. It was "The Halfling Song."

Neal, my brother, the Dungeon Master from our earliest gaming days, hated halflings. I loved them and often played them in our games, and so he almost unilaterally hated my characters. I delighted in tormenting him with the characters almost as much as he delighted in tormenting me with his reactions to them. We were young, and we were brothers, and such a dynamic is not uncommon. There, seated with our few friends around the kitchen table in a threadbare trailer home in the late hours of a summer evening with no air conditioning, arguing as adolescent boys do about who had farted, my character was confronted in a tavern by a lizard man accusing my character of passing gas in said tavern and insisting that my character sing and dance by way of recompense. So you see, it was all my brother's fault. I was playing a halfling thief named Toho Fuzzboll, and me being who I was (even way back then,) I immediately burst out into "The Halfling Song."

I will not utter the words here, though I cannot rule out the possibility that, at some convention in the future, deep in my cups and plied with further libation, I might be coerced into recounting them for you. An appropriately interesting offer might—*might*—even get me to sing it for you, but probably not on both counts. As it is, you should simply imagine a silly, semi-nonsensical, very slightly profane, rollicking and short tune about halflings and bodily functions and drinking. In all actuality this paragraph and that description was longer, more impressive, and less embarrassing than the song itself. Back to the 1980s, and our game...

At the table, I sang; ergo Toho also sang in the tavern within the game. Our friends, caught off guard by both my lack of hesitation and enthusiastic singing, fell into peals of sleep-deprived laughter. My brother wasn't as amused but did smile as he told me the lizard man was swinging his sword. Although Toho was a low-level PC and quite likely to die in this encounter, the lizard man missed with his attack. My brother would not let me draw my sword and attack in the same round and no other players stepped to my defense. Pressed for Toho's next action, I opted to bite the lizard man, causing everyone at the table to laugh once again.

I rolled a 20.

Toho latched on to the lizard man's calf with his teeth and even with the natural 20 did a negligible amount of damage. The lizard man swung his sword at Toho again. Neal rolled a 1. Uncharacteristically, probably intoxicated by the laughter around the table, my brother decided that this would count as a double-damage hit by the lizard man against himself, and then proceeded to roll the maximum amount of damage possible. It was a perfect dice-storm. The lizard man cut off his own leg and bled to death on the tavern floor. Toho spat out a bloody chunk of lizard flesh and washed it down with the remainder of the lizard man's own ale, and then proceeded to the bar top to sing "The Halfling Song" once again.

Our friends cheered. Even my brother laughed. A (very small) legend was born, and "The Halfling Song" continued to be sung for a few years, although at intervals of increasing irregularity, until it passed out of our gaming existence and went to live in that vast, decrepit storehouse of memories in my head that I generally only visit on accident. But the seed that would eventually grow into my vocation was planted that night, around a gaming table, in that mid-1980's summer heat of the trailer park.

The sense of humor I honed around that gaming table, and many others, somehow grew into a musical stand-up comedy career a couple of decades later, and I found myself traveling the country, singing my silly, rollicking, oftentimes profane songs to middle America. Granted, there were no halflings or lizard men.

I performed on NBC multiple times (on a regional television show you won't have heard of, but NBC, nonetheless). I performed in 38 states, at the Atlantis Resort in the Bahamas, multiple times each at the House of Blues and the Hard Rock Casino. I performed at bars and in theaters, in comedy clubs and bowling allies, dance halls, Moose Lodges, Eagles Lodges, American Legions, and even in a sushi restaurant once. I slept in rest areas and four-star hotels and pretty much everywhere in between. I visited cheap roadside attractions, used bookstores, and craft breweries to stave off the boredom of life on the road. That's what turns performers into addicts, you know: boredom and loneliness.

For too much of that time there was no gaming. Growing up and incurring responsibilities has a way of eliminating (or at the least markedly limiting) your availability for games and gaming even when you aren't traveling the country for work. But as I was spending large amounts of time driving, I began to listen to podcasts to pass the time. I tried listening to a few 'actual play' podcasts (where you listen to a group of other people game) but they were mostly infuriating. I found that all the goofing off around a table felt much less fun if I wasn't part of it, and it didn't take long to realize they weren't for me in general. So, I sought out podcasts about role playing games that didn't include a live gameplay portion, but instead discussed the theory and practice of playing the games, how to have better games, be a better player, a better game master. I found a couple that I liked well enough, but they'd already folded by the time I started listening, and didn't have many episodes to begin with.

Then I found *Fear The Boot*. It was an active podcast, still putting out episodes, and I immediately dug in and decided that these were people I could enjoy playing games with, and actively wanted to do so. I was on the road, devouring episodes at an insane pace. In early December of 2008, I became overjoyed upon hearing that they'd organized a gaming convention/game day called Fear The Con, and then just as quickly crushed when I realized it had happened over the previous summer. I'd missed it. I burned through the next year's worth of episodes, getting myself current on the podcast and realizing they were planning a second convention for the following March. I reached out to them and before I knew it, I was not only going to get to game again, but I'd be gaming with these people I'd formed an attachment to by being a fan of their podcast, and I'd also be performing for them at the convention.

March 2009 couldn't come fast enough. When the weekend of the convention arrived I was both nervous and excited. It was odd... I'd stopped being nervous before shows years before, but something about this was different, and I knew it. There were six four-hour-long gaming slots that made up the convention, spread out over two days. For the first of the six slots, I did nothing but lurk and watch. I signed up for games in four of the other slots, though, and had an incredible time. And then I performed in front of a full crowd of gamers who greeted me with open arms as one of their own, even though my act wasn't geeky at all, in fact it never even so much as mentioned gaming. I remember a couple of guys helping me carry my gear out of the convention hall and load it back into my car. I offered them t-shirts as a gesture of thanks, but neither of my t-shirts were to their tastes (I had one shirt that read "It's a Licky Licky Night" and another with an ambigram that read "Yes Dear" upright and "Fuck You" upside down,) so they politely declined. It was then, that moment, that inter-action, that made me want to have specific material for conventions, for geeks, for the vast extended geek family I hadn't even known I wanted, let alone stepped in the midst of.

Over the next year, I played board games at home with my kids and did shows and even started occasionally gaming while on the road with friends I'd met through being a fan of the podcast, through the online forums and in person at the convention. March 2010 came, and I performed at Fear The Con again, and my bond with that group of awesome folks strengthened, but I still hadn't acted on that urge to write songs expressing my geeky side, the side of me in love with fantasy and science fiction, video and role-playing games, cartoons, books, and movies.

That July, Dan Repperger and a group of people from around the country, literally from several different states, (Michigan, Minnesota, Missouri, North Carolina, and Pennsylvania off the top of my head, a crowd of around 20 or so geeks) converged on Fort Wayne, IN to watch me perform at Snickerz Comedy Bar. They made such a fuss over me that the feature act—the middle act—of the show, Mike Bobbitt (a funny comic and certifiable geek in his own right), might have thought I was a bigger deal than I was. They bought expensive beers from local stores and we laughed and talked and drank, and I felt like a star. The next week, however, I was right back on the road, slinging and singing dick jokes to a receptive, though decidedly mundane audience at Jokerz Comedy Club in Milwaukee, WI. It just wasn't the same.

But in March 2011, I released a song and video that went viral ("She Don't Like Firefly") and performed it for the first time ever at

Fear The Con 4 in St. Louis, MO. It changed the trajectory of my career.

The reaction made me realize there was an audience for the geeky side of me, not just playing to the lowest common denominator, but being able to write songs about the things that connect with me on a deeper and more personal level: role playing games, science fiction, fantasy, video games, superheroes, books, and all the random minutiae that filled up my shelves at home. There was an audience I could be unapologetically silly and weird (and a little profane) for.

I'm tempted to say I found my tribe, at the risk of being guilty of cultural appropriation. Without a doubt, however, I'd found my new, geeky extended family.

2

SIDE QUESTS

I like video games. I know that's not uncommon, but I'm particular about the video games I play. In my early twenties, I bought a PlayStation (way back before they were call PS Ones) because my brother let me start playing *Final Fantasy VII* at his house one night in the mid-90s and everything changed. I didn't have a gaming group, and video game RPGs (role-playing games, not rocket-propelled grenades) might not be tabletop RPGs by a long shot, and seem pretty limited in many regards in comparison with tabletop RPGs, but that doesn't mean they're not enjoyable or fulfilling in different ways.

I like video games with sandbox-style worlds where the characters can roam and explore and follow side quests and mini games. I was talking with my oldest about a trip to a used game store a few years ago and told him I'd brought home a few new (to me) video games. He asked me what I came home with, so I listed them off: *Red Dead Redemption II, Witcher III: The Wild Hunt, Brutal Legend,* and *Destiny 2.* He called them *Skyrim* on a Horse, *Skyrim* with Faerie Tales and Sex Scenes, *Skyrim* with Rock Music, and *Skyrim* in Space. I guess he had a point. I've long loved the *Grand Theft Auto* Games, the *Final Fantasy* Games, and of course *Skyrim.* You could say I have a type.

But for the most part, following the main story line is something I do to get access to areas I can't reach without progressing in the game. For me, the exploration is the fun part—that and the mini games and dressing up my character in new gear like a digital Barbie doll, because accessorizing is fun as hell. When I run out of side quests in video games, I make my own. For example, in *Grand Theft Auto* games, I like to collect all the safe houses. I like to buy new clothes and get haircuts and tattoos and accessories and cars that I like. I don't care nearly as much about the storyline as I do about driving around, getting my character to look the way I want them to, and listening to the radio stations.

In *Skyrim*, I always avoid going to the Jarl's place in Whiterun when I start a new character. You can avoid almost, if not all random dragon attacks that way; and be level 99 by the time you start the main quest line if you want. At one point I made an effort to steal every sweet roll I could find, just because of a guard's dialog, the one where he says, "Let me guess. Somebody stole your sweet roll?" It was senseless, silly fun, as sweet rolls are all over the game, they have no weight, and you can store dozens—hundreds? thousands?—of them in a chest or bag in any of your homes.

I like the *Hearthfire* expansion that lets you build houses. It's a mini game that runs right up my alley. Gathering construction materials, building the homes, and then decorating them. I spent a month or so playing *Skyrim*, off and on, with a reference sheet, collecting all 15 copies (actually, I think there might have been more) of one particular book for a bookshelf in my library, and both copies of another book that you can find. That's right: on two shelves set aside in my library, I had every available copy of *The Lusty Argonian Maid*, and both extant copies of *The Sultry Argonian Bard*. I installed the *Dawnguard* and *Dragonborn* expansion packs just to get them all. I fought cultists and vampires because I found some bizarre joy in collecting virtual copies of a non-existent, naughty book in a video game.

That's the point, right? To have fun, to keep it interesting, to make the content engaging for you, which is what I was doing in the games.

I do it professionally, too. I set up side quests, things that I think are interesting to me, and hope that they pan out in some way that is beneficial, or at least not detrimental, to my career. I did a podcast called Beer Powered Time Machine because I liked trying new beers and telling stories with my friends. I take on creative projects like writing the *American Gods*-inspired EP *Storm Coming*, or doing the *In The 'Verse* Podcast with Marc Gunn, watching every episode of *Firefly*, analyzing it and writing a song inspired by something in each episode. I enjoyed it so much we started a second season with different media: Doctor Who and *The Hobbit* and more. Once, I wrote an album's worth of punk songs about cats. Come to think of it, my entire current career is comprised completely of side quests.

It could be considered a side quest in itself, or at least the product of one, because it began as a side gig, a passion project, when I was a full-time standup comedian, touring the country and beyond, slinging jokes and funny music and babysitting drunks. But then I wrote and recorded a video and a song called "She Don't Like Firefly," which went viral and showed me that there was an audience for these things I cared about.

That was in 2011. By 2017, six geek albums and a couple of EPs later, I was doing geek entertainment full time at conventions and online, and only doing standup as a part-time gig to fill in the gaps. In 2019, I retired from standup altogether, because of the side quest. Because the side quests aren't just a distraction, they're the real content that fills up your life, the moments and hours between the big events and the big plans, even the idea of accomplishing those big plans, of making the big events happen, it all usually involves dozens of side quests in addition to what we'd consider the "main storyline" quests. Remember, life is the ultimate sandbox RPG: completely customizable, to the extent that you can afford to do it and/or the lengths you are willing go in order to make it happen.

Remember those silly dreams you had as a kid? Want a big unicorn mural in your home? You're an adult now. You can do that. A van with a bitching wizard on the side? Totally achievable. A classy bar in your living room? A large library in your home, decorated just so? A themed gaming room? These all sound like side quests to me. Just figure out what you need to do to get that first copy of *The Lusty Argonian Maid* and get to work.

She Don't Like Firefly

She's got a good job, she works hard for the money.
    She looks like a model, like a Playboy Bunny.
    She likes comic books and video games,
    She even plays Warhammer 40K.

But she don't like *Firefly*. That's why I had to say goodbye.
    No, she don't like *Firefly*, so she's gone, gone, gone.

She drinks good beer, she drives a hybrid car,
    She's hotter than her Warcraft avatar.
    She's got her own dice bag for role-playing games.
    She even wears steampunk lingerie...

But she don't like *Firefly*. She didn't even cry when Wash died.
    No, she don't like *Firefly*, so she's gone, gone, gone.

For our one-month anniversary
    We spent a weekend naked playing Halo 3.
    We had a great time laughing at zombie movies,
    'Til I pulled out my copy of *Serenity*.
    She got all tense, said, "Do we have to watch this?"
    I just said, "Xiao Jie! Hit the bricks!"

'Cause she don't like *Firefly*. She didn't even cry when Wash died.
    No, she don't like *Firefly*, so she's gone, gone, gone.
    No she don't like *Firefly*. That's why I had to say goodbye.
    No, she don't like *Firefly*, so she's gone, gone, gone.

3

SHE DON'T LIKE FIREFLY

When, in September of 2002, that plucky little space western *Firefly* premiered, I watched it. At least I tried to. I'd set my VCR to record it and everything. I loved sci-fi, and although I wasn't a fan of *Buffy the Vampire Slayer* or Joss Whedon's work in general, I was always on board to give new sci-fi a shot. But the show just didn't click with me. I like to think it was because they aired the episodes out of order, and I never saw the pilot episode until years later, the one that hooks you on the 'Verse and the characters that populated it, but at the time I was just… confused. So, I didn't even try to watch another episode, not for a long time.

Not, at least, until my friend Ty Morton insisted that I give it another try and loaned me his boxed set. It was fall of 2008, and his DVDs remained on a shelf in my living room for a few months without ever having been opened, let alone watched. I even took them with me to the Bahamas for 2 weeks when I worked at the Atlantis Resort and Casino, figuring I could give it a shot on my computer in the hotel room, but it turns out that, at the time I visited the Bahamas, a bottle of water was $4, a can of soda was $3.50, but a pint of rum (and they had many, many flavors of rum) was a mere $1.77. Those numbers remain somehow emblazoned in my mind, although much of my time in the Bahamas is sadly not. Suffice it to say, I didn't watch the show there. I think.

In December, near Christmas, Ty asked if I was ever going to return his DVDs, and I asked him for just one more shot at watching it. On December twenty-fifth, 2008, I watched the first three episodes. By the time I had reached, "Curse your sudden but inevitable betrayal" in the pilot episode, I was a fan. It was a bona fide Christmas Miracle™.

The song, however, wasn't written until February of 2011. I sang the rough idea for the chorus and some of the verse into my phone's voice memo recorder while I drove home on February 16th, the day after a Tuesday night gig at Tipper's in Clarksville, TN. It's a habit I have so I don't lose ideas, potential lyrics, or melodies when I'm driving. By the next day, the first version of the song had been recorded. It had slightly different lyrics than the final version and it sounded like Alabama was singing it (the country group, not the state. Well... maybe the state). I didn't feel quite like it was what I wanted. It didn't quite match the 'Comedy Rock Star' image I had tried to culti-vate on comedy club stages, so I figured I'd let it gestate.

Later in the week, I was working in Johnson City, TN and have the distinct memory of walking through the Holiday Inn from my room to the nearby staircase in the moments after the inspiration for the revised melody and style hit me. (Sort of like Nickelback, if you pressed me to describe it, though this was before the vox populi decided Nickelback was the punchline to a joke.) I was singing it as I walked down the hall, knowing other hotel guests were looking at me as if I was insane, and I laughed out loud as I entered the stairwell. There is an elation attached to figuring out the solution to a persistent and perplexing artistic problem that is difficult to describe, but I can only imagine it's akin to the painful joy of passing a kidney stone. There's a lot of sweat, tears, agony, and effort leading up to one crucial moment, after which there is mostly relief and exultation.

So, I went home and recorded that version—the rock version—sometime in the next two weeks, between shows across Michigan and Ohio. I don't know the exact date, but I do know it had been finished by Sunday, March 6, because that was the date of the video shoot. We shot most of it at Ty Morton's house, and a friend of his, Kerry Anne, agreed to come help. The video came together faster than you might imagine. Kerry Anne and Ty were enthusiastic, patient, and helpful as we rearranged his furniture and set up lights to get certain shots. They took direction, made suggestions, and maintained a genuinely cheerful mood as we worked.

After we finished at Ty's place, we went to the pub to shoot the opening sequence and get a beer before it opened to the public. We got there later than expected, and setting up took longer than we thought too, so by the time we were ready to shoot the bar was already opening. Luckily, everyone was cool about it, and stayed quiet at the other end of the bar while I lip-synched to a video camera set up opposite me between the beer towers while the song played on my phone, kept just out of frame. I only got one take of that shot, but it was enough. We tore down the equipment, drank our beers, and went home.

Before I continue with the story of "She Don't Like Firefly," here are some answers to some of the most frequently asked questions about the video: The woman's name is Kerry Anne. No, I won't tell you her last name. Yes, she is a geek. The bar in the video is the Fickle Peach in Muncie, IN. Yes, those are her legs in that shot in the video. The bartender was played by Ty Morton, the very man who introduced me to *Firefly*. No she's not single. Yes, I still go the Fickle Peach on a weekly basis, if not more often. The beer in our glasses (mine and Kerry Anne's) was Three Floyd's Pride and Joy. Yes, she is married. Yes, they're happy together. No, I still won't tell you her last name —*whatiswrongwithyou?!*

The video was edited and posted on YouTube the next day, Monday, March 7, 2011, and it didn't seem like that much of a big deal until the next day, when my life took a bit of a left turn. At about 2 in the afternoon on Tuesday the 8th, @dreuters tweeted the video link at Nathan Fillion, Jewel Staite, and Morena Baccarin, asking if they'd seen it. Morena Baccarin responded within minutes, retweeting it with "Soooo great!!" Jewel Staite and Adam Baldwin retweeted the song, as did Alan Tudyk's brother. (Alan wasn't on Twitter at the time.) And, just like that, I had a viral video.

Time Magazine's tech.tv mentioned it, and linked to it in their "Going Viral" section, it was featured in a small story on Nerdist.com, and SyFy's Blastr.com. In fact, every 15 minutes my phone would buzz with anywhere between a hundred and a thousand new views (I had my push notifications turned on. Being successful was a bit of a novelty for me). I kept my phone on the bedside table and woke up several times through the night, looking at the screen to see the new number of views, sometimes taking a screenshot.

What made it more surreal was that Jody (my wife) and I had planned a weekend-long family mini-vacation to Brown County with our sons, where we stayed a couple nights at a lodge with a water park in it. We wanted to spend some time on vacation where I wasn't working, but as the video continued to go viral, I started making phone calls and planning other projects and videos, and it turned out that I ended up working through most of those couple of days anyway while we hiked with the boys, or poolside while the three of them enjoyed the water park. It drastically changed the dynamic of the trip, but they were, as they always have been, very understanding.

The next weekend I attended and performed at Fear The Con IV in St. Louis, MO, a convention that had taken me in as a traveling dick joke comic and purveyor of risqué t-shirts and welcomed me into their community anyway. I had already performed at two of their conventions with no geek material to speak of. This time, I came armed with "She Don't Like Firefly" and dreams for an entire geek rock comedy album. I performed the song and they sang along and cheered. It was exactly the kind of connection I'd hoped for since that moment loading the car after Fear The Con II—something that touched the pulse of geekdom, but was still me, still my act. I talked about my plans for the future album, and they cheered. And when the time came to fund the album on Kickstarter, they backed it.

Having a video go viral doesn't mean an instant change in fame or lifestyle. I imagine it might in some instances, but most of the time it just provides a measure of attention that, if leveraged properly, can be built into something else. I'm not sure I leveraged the viral nature of the song to its full potential. I was just figuring things out as I went at the time, but "She Don't Like Firefly" opened the door for me to find what I was meant to do, to transition from singing dick jokes to middle America to singing slightly more intellectual penis jokes to geeks at conventions. I'm joking, of course, but it marked a definite change in my trajectory.

When I began recording the *Impotent Nerd Rage* album in summer of 2011, the first song I tracked was "She Don't Like Firefly." I laid down all the instrument tracks and came back to do vocals on it after I'd tracked the instruments for the next song, but when I sang it, I came to the realization that I'd recorded it a bit too slow. Not quite slow like a 45 RPM record being played at 33 RPM, but just slow enough to feel sedated. (Some younger readers may have to do some light research to get that reference, but there's an easy fix. Just ask anyone who loves vinyl records, or anyone born before the mid-1980s.) I had to redo the entire thing so it didn't feel sluggish, which took up studio time and annoyed the recording engineer, Frank. He was very patient with me, however, after realizing it was my first time in a studio, and he is a huge part of why *Impotent Nerd Rage* sounds so good.

Not everyone had such a positive reaction to the song, though. One guy loved it and showed it to his girlfriend who got upset because she'd just started loving *Firefly*, but hadn't seen the movie, and then blamed *me* in the comments on the video for spoiling the movie for her. He wrote, "Fuck you, man. Ruined it for her..." Me? *I* ruined it for her? I didn't even know his girlfriend. He's the one that showed her the video, right?

At the time, I quoted a tweet from Nathan Fillion, "If it's about last season, it ain't a spoiler--you be behind da times." I was being called out for releasing a song in 2011 containing a spoiler for a movie released on DVD in 2005, and I took it personally. Look, I admit that it might have been a less than diplomatic response. I read the comments and got butthurt and reacted. For a couple of years, I would rant about it onstage at performances, saying things like, "I don't want to ruin things for you, so if you're spoiler averse stop listening now, but Darth Vader is Luke's father, Snape kills Dumbledore, Soylent Green is people, and the Cat in the Hat turns out to be a walrus in a corset. For a while a spoiler is a spoiler. After enough time it becomes ingrained as a cultural touchstone."

A few years later, though, I distinctly remembered playing a game of Trivial Pursuit with my family back when I was a teenager. My grandma had asked me the question, "Who cut off Luke Skywalker's hand?"

I answered, "His father."

"Wrong," she said. "It was Darth Vader." Despite all my pleas and protestations, I could not convince my grandmother that Darth Vader was Luke's father. She hadn't seen the movies and, moreover, didn't care.

Everyone else at the table laughed and agreed with me, but since I was winning, sided with her. They decided I had to answer the question in a way the questioner would accept or whatever. Yes, I'm still pissy about it. Never played with them again, but that's beside the point. The point is that what we believe are cultural touchstones, and things that might, indeed, *be* cultural touchstones to us aren't always known to everyone. In recent years and after much consideration, I've become a kindler, gentler comedy rock geek, and haven't wanted to accidentally spoil it for anyone. When I perform the song now, I sing, "She didn't even cry when SPOILERS," or "She didn't even cry when REDACTED." It gets a great laugh, especially among those who know my long and contentious relationship with some folks' reactions to that line. This pleases me to no end, but I'm still pissed about that Trivial Pursuit game.

Mostly, however, the negative comments missed the fact that the video and the song were a joke, somehow seeming to believe that this video was a documentary of sorts wherein I, a portly comedian of dubious looks and charms, connected with a gorgeous woman with a great job, an unquestionable reserve of patience, and similar interests in every single area except one: the appreciation of a television show that aired twelve of its fourteen episodes before being cancelled in

2003. Upon discovering this I then broke up with her, wrote and recorded a rock song about the experience, got her to come back into the home, lip sync the lyrics for a video shoot, relive the good times and the ultimate breakup, and then edited it together and put it online. All it is missing is narration by David Attenborough.

Eventually this all convinced me to stop reading the comments. The praise is great, but if people connect with and appreciate what you're making, they'll support you. They'll share it. They'll buy it. They'll proselytize for it. And if they don't? Well... Every comment and every play, even plays from people who don't like it and comments from people who are insulting you, even who seem to hate you, just increases the odds that someone else will see it. For my mental health, I tend not to read them anymore. It's my opinion that you shouldn't accept the praise if you're not willing to accept the criticism, and while I'm willing to do both, I think both praise and criticism should be given in a way that is both honest and kind.

If you can't do that, then get bent or something.

Grab a poker, stoke the fire, get the water nice and hot.

Cut the onions, the potatoes, throw them all into the pot.

But it seems like something's missing in this bubbling vat of gravy...

From the village square a woman screams, "Kobolds Ate My Baby!"

Kobolds ate my baby, for Torg—All Hail King Torg!

Bar all the windows and lock all the doors, cause kobolds are hunting tonight.

They want a sweet little human treat, and a baby will do just right.

In honor of Vor, the Big Angry Red God, their ruler has declared a feast

Of succulent pastries and dainty delights, and exotic delicacies. (That means babies!)

Kobolds ate my baby, for Torg—All Hail King Torg!

They're short and they're hairy and so full of teeth, their mouth takes up most of their
head.

Stupid and hungry, and tasty as well, most of them soon end up dead.

But quicker than tribbles or rabbits can mate, they repopulate with ease.

And so, to avoid being thrown in the pot, they gear up and hunt babies. (Catch that baby!)

Kobolds ate my baby, for Torg—All Hail King Torg!

Kobolds eat a bunch of different things, disgusting and delicious.
   They don't care if it is fattening or cardboard or nutritious.
   But they'll pass up almost anything to grab a little baby,
   And the reason they like babies best is "'cause babies is so tasty!"

Kobolds ate my baby, for Torg—All Hail King Torg!

4

KOBOLDS ATE MY BABY

The idea for this song came to me shortly after hearing about the Ninth Level Games "beer and pretzels RPG" of the same name. Wait--that's not completely true. I'd heard of the game a year before the song hit my head. I had attended Fear The Con II in St. Louis, Missouri, and heard people talking about playing this game after hours. I thought it sounded great, but it got lost in the shuffle of performing at the con and the daily grind of life as a road comic. So my subconscious, if I were to be honest, had a good year to stew over it and work something up. In the spring of 2010, I was gearing up to attend Fear The Con III, and discussions on the online chat boards for the Fear The Boot podcast brought the game to my attention again. That's when the song came to me.

The staccato, rhythmic intro and chorus appeared almost intact in my head. (Seriously... within ten to fifteen minutes of reading about the game again, I had this chunk of song in my head.) I set about buying the game from eBay sellers (an original edition—saddle-stapled card stock over copy paper, all in black and white—and a Super Deluxe Edition) and read them for context and material to use so I could write a cohesive song about them. I'd wished it would've been ready for Fear the Con III, but it wasn't. Nothing geeky was. I hadn't even given serious consideration to making geeky music yet. I mean... the thought was there, the desire, but I wasn't ready to give up the standup comedy ghost—wasn't sure I even could—for a long while.

There are songs from my standup act that popped up on albums because I wanted to fill them out and hadn't yet got into the swing of making new music ALL THE TIME, all the way up until, and including, the *Tentacow* album. So yeah, "She Don't Like Firefly" changed everything, but although the shift in mental perspective seemed instant, knowing what I wanted to work towards, the actual process of shifting careers and material was extremely slow and gradual by comparison.

I went through a long period of time waffling and bouncing back and forth between the idea of combining my two acts, the standup comedy and the geeky comedy, into an amalgam of both with the best components of each; the idea of converting my main act into geek comedy, shifting the tone and content of the whole thing; the thought that I'd maintain separate careers in standup and geeky comedy. So the standup songs—even ones I'd rather not be associated with anymore—kept finding their way onto my albums. But "She Don't Like Firefly", in a very real sense, changed everything.

I'd been holding this idea of an all-geek-material act in my head and knew this song would have to be a part of it. When the decision was made to write and record the *Impotent Nerd Rage* album, and once the Kickstarter was funded, this was the next original song I set about completing. (I flirted with a couple of parodies, first-- "If I Had A Mutant Power" and "Smells Like Team Justice," but I have a complicated relationship with parodies that I'll discuss later, likely at length. Possibly repetitively.) The rest of the song didn't come as easily as the first chunks, but it did come.

I found that the real key to finishing the song, to understanding the material, was in playing the game with my gaming group. I had been regularly playing RPGs again for a while with Ty Morton, Randy Davis, Sean Smith, and Ty's son, William. We took a night off from our regular campaign, I rolled up a stack of pre-generated kobold characters, and we spent a night playing *Kobolds Ate My Baby*. We made silly voices and drank beer (those of us who were of age, that is), and had a raucous good time as they tried to steal babies from a farmhouse, helped each other, turned on each other, made valiant stands and died horrible deaths or ran away. It was a glorious night of gaming, and when it came time to shout the choruses of, "All Hail King Torg," I asked them come into the studio to shout them with me. You can hear them on the album, and my partner Jody was the voice of the "screaming village woman" at the beginning of the song.

An interesting side note: When recording the song, Frank (Reber, the recording engineer) could hear something was off somehow and poked his head into the recording area. He saw how I was standing and told me something along the lines of, "You're singing like Dio, you need to be standing like Dio when you sing it!" So I did. I found that felt better, I connected to the main melody of the song when I was making grand, melodramatic gestures, feet planted far apart, and that somehow translated into the recording. Jody told me she could hear it in the vocals, somehow. I hope you can, too. It's a fun, catchy tune. Frank said that recording this song was like recording a radio play, with all the voices and everything.

Performing the song has always brought an interesting response. It's fun to explain why you're asking people to shout, "All hail King Torg!" and it's fun for them to do. It's an easy way to draw an audience in and make them feel like they belong with each other and with you, that everyone is part of a great whole. But it doesn't always work. There are always some people who just don't want to participate, for whatever reason, or who don't get it. And that's okay. Sometimes there's nothing you can do about it. Sometimes you can pull them around to your side, and that feels incredible.

I don't remember where it was, but I was playing a convention and a young girl was there with her parents, not yet old enough for middle school, and she looked concerned while I was singing, not like she was going to cry, but very much like something was bothering her, so I stopped and asked if she was okay, and she said, in a loud and matter-of-fact manner, "You should Not. Eat. Babies. It's wrong."

Everyone laughed, but her face didn't change, so I told her, "No babies were harmed in the making of this song. Kobolds are just for pretend, and so when we pretend to be kobolds, we pretend to eat pretend babies. Okay?" And she smiled and nodded and I started back into the chorus and she became the loudest little kobold in the room. Everyone cheered far harder than they'd laughed. She was one of us.

Speaking of babies, have I mentioned that I saved a baby once at DragonCon? True story. Sort of. I was setting up to perform at the AmericasMart concourse, near the three stories of vendor halls, when I heard the very distinct sound of a small child wailing around the corner, near the elevators. When I got there, a family had been getting into the elevator (a mom, dad, infant and a toddler). The toddler had his hand on the sliding metal door and, as it opened, his hand was pulled with it and wedged into the door. The elevator was dinging, the mom was holding the baby, the toddler was crying, and the dad was frantically trying to pull the child's arm free. Geek bard to the rescue.

"Hold on," I said, and grabbed the side of the door, pulling it toward me to make more space to pull the toddler's arm free. I didn't see who, but someone was helping me pull. I'm pretty sure it was John Panzarella, a fixture of the concourse stages at DragonCon, who was setting up the sound for my show that afternoon. As we pulled the door toward us, shifting the weight off the toddler's arm, the father was able to free the trapped arm and they piled out of the elevator. Mom and Dad were checking on the toddler, as was John's wife, Kathy—a registered nurse—and seeing that everything was under control I went back and finished setting up for my show. The last thing they needed was one more onlooker in the way, and I had a soundcheck to do.

Later on in the weekend, I'd popped down to the Hyatt Concourse to catch the last-ever DragonCon show of Emerald Rose, a fantastic Celtic music group that had decided to make that year their last as a band. It was standing room only around the small stage area, people pressed shoulder to shoulder, singing and clapping along. Clyde Gilbert, the bassist (and director of the DragonCon concourse stages) saw me in the audience and called me out from the microphone.

"Mikey Mason," he said. "I see you out there. I know what you did."

It was ominous sounding. People were laughing. I felt like a kid who'd been called out in front of the class.

"I didn't do anything," I said. "It wasn't me." Everyone laughed some more.

"You saved a baby," Clyde said, and I shook my head as people started to whoop and cheer in the concourse.

"I did not save a baby…"

"Yes, you did," said Clyde. "John told me. He saw the whole thing. You saved a baby at the AmericasMart today." A hush came over the crowded concourse, droves of people staring at me expectantly, and it felt like the whole of existence was being held in the sheer gravity of the moment, waiting on my next words.

"I… I saved a baby," I muttered, shrugging and nodding my head, and the whole place went up in a cheer so loud you'd have thought I saved THEIR babies. Clyde smiled, Emerald Rose launched into a high-energy song, and I was clapped on the shoulders by people all around. The rest of their show was amazing, as usual. Afterwards, Clyde wanted me to know that he'd make sure what I'd done would be heard about higher up.

The funny part? I'd forgotten it happened until Clyde brought it up at that show. When he first uttered the words, "I know what you did," I thought for certain I was never going to be allowed back at DragonCon again for something that I didn't even know about. Look, it's great to feel like a hero, but it feels just as good, maybe even better, to know you haven't trashed your entire career somehow without even realizing it. That's a feeling that's hard to beat, and it took a few minutes before my balls dropped back down from my body cavity.

But back to the song…

When Chris O'Neill, one of the creative duo behind the *Kobolds Ate My Baby!* role playing game, found out about the song, he flipped out (in a good way) and asked to use it for the *Kobolds Ate My Baby! in Color* Kickstarter. I agreed without hesitation and have since been treated to many videos of large groups of people at conventions singing the song with him. We kept trying to meet up at various conventions over the years, but kept just missing each other.

The meeting did happen, though. At Origins in October of 2019 (it was my first Origins, Chris's 25th or so) I helped kick off their Midnight Massacre in the Taft Room. There were 100-150 people seated, ready to play kobolds itching to get their grubby little hands on babies or die trying, and many, if not most of them had heard my song. So, when Chris introduced me, the cheer that went up was more heartening than I'd have thought possible. I began to prowl the room with my acoustic guitar, beginning the song. There was no sound equipment, so I was projecting as loud as I could, summoning every ounce of busking skill I could, and when I sang that first, "For Torg," what followed was the unforgettable, epic roar of a hundred-plus late-night gamers around tables screaming, "ALL HAIL KING TORG!" like the battle cry from a fantasy movie.

If you've ever wondered what it might be like, being a bard in a fantasy world, playing a song and lending bardic inspiration to a field of warriors about to charge the battlefield, this is about as close as I think it gets. The energy was palpable as I moved among the tables, looking from player to player, seeing them smile, knowing what was coming, feeling their anticipation and the sheer exultation of letting ourselves be swept away in a moment of expressing our mutual excitement for something we love. The roar was so loud I literally, physically felt it. I sang my heart out, they screamed their hearts out.

It was more than just the definition of awesome. I'd found my horde.

5

MY PARODY PROBLEM

I have a complicated relationship with parodies.

For a guy who doesn't do a lot of parodies, I seem to do a lot of parodies. I mean, percentage-wise, that's just not true. If you look at the numbers, and being the guy I am, I *have*, approximately ninety-five percent of the music in my official releases are original songs, not parodic in nature, and that's not even taking into consideration the number of songs I write or have written that haven't made it onto an album yet (and maybe won't). So you might be able to see why I chafe a little bit at my songs being called parodies. It's nothing personal, it's just... entirely personal.

I find it weird that many people seem to associate me with parodies for the sole reason that I am a musician who writes and performs funny or geeky music, but that speaks more to their internal assumptions and biases than it does to my body of work. It does tend to make me shy away even more from doing parodies, though. My friend Madison "Metricula" Roberts suffers a different version of the same problem. Because she's a woman, people often assume she's playing a ukulele, even back when she didn't own one, and people who have seen her perform LIVE still assume she's playing a ukulele—really—despite the fact that she plays a full-size acoustic guitar, and the more people who make that assumption, the less inclined I think she feels towards ever playing one on stage. Similarly, people who have sat through entire shows of mine where not a single parody was performed will still sometimes call my music parodies. It's a personal issue I grapple with. Anyway...

You can't discuss parodies without Weird Al coming up, so let's start there. I know, I know... He's an incredible performer. He's a great musician. He plays a killer accordion. He travels with an incredible band. I can't and won't argue with any of that. But most of the world doesn't care about his best work. Most of the world just admires him for his parodies. I don't. Why?

Here's where I'm about to risk losing popularity and goodwill (especially with a lot of my fellow comedians and performers, and please remember this is coming from a guy who does the occasional parody, himself): Without question, writing a parody objectively takes less skill, talent, and work than writing a catchy, popular song (or even a not-so-catchy, not-so-popular, not-so-good song, for that matter). It's true.

Very few people write parodies of lesser-known songs by artists (though it happens) or parodies of a demo song by a famous musician that didn't make it to an album. They most often pick songs that you already know and either love or hate. Either way, you're already a little invested in the song and they don't have to do most of the work to make you pay attention. If you like the original song, you'll listen to the parody because of that. If you hate the original song, you'll listen to the parody because you want to hear it twisted. Either way, the parodist has most of the work already done before they even start *their* part. The listener goes into the experience already knowing the melody and maybe the words, and if they know the words to the original song, they can probably guess many of the lyrics that will be used in the parody. The parody goes in already owning mental real estate in your head, whether you want it or not, mental real estate that the parodist didn't have to work for in the least.

Writing a song requires arranging chord structures, creating a melody, and writing lyrics. It involves tempo, mood, pacing, instrument choice, and even a sense of the theatrical. Well-written songs stick in your head; they're ear worms. Sometimes you don't even like the song, but you can't get it out of your head, anyway. That means it was well-written (note, I was careful to avoid using the word 'good.' I'm trying to stay objective), and that's not even scratching the surface of whether or how the song will be marketed.

Writing a parody requires that you take a song that somebody else already did all of that for, including the marketing, and re-writing the lyrics. That's it. Done. A parody purposefully cashes in on someone else's hard work and talent and the exposure of a popular song.

"Wait," you argue. "But Weird Al is talented and does it very well and has socially relevant lyrics and is an incredible performer and reproduces the music with an almost inhuman attention to detail and blahblahblah..."

And I'll stop you right there, because it's all beside the point. The point is that writing lyrics is only one part of writing a song. And writing parody lyrics doesn't even involve creating a rhyme scheme or meter. That part is already done for you as well.

See? Writing a song takes an incredible amount of work and skill and talent, and writing lyrics is a single part of that. When you take a song that somebody else put in all the time and effort on, and re-write the lyrics, even if you do it well, you've still done a mere fraction of the work. Writing a complete song is harder than just writing lyrics, if only because writing a complete song takes a wider skill set than just writing lyrics.

Leave subjective terms like "good" or "bad" out of it. I'm talking about the work and talents and skills involved, and writing a song is more sheer work and utilizes more talents and skills (and therefore is more difficult) than just writing lyrics. It follows logically then, that writing a parody is less work than writing a song and requires less talent or skill.

Which is why Weird Al makes me a little sad. His original music (mostly pastiches—songs that imitate a particular style or artist without parodying a specific song), the stuff he put ALL of the work in on, is the least acclaimed of his works. "One More Minute" is a killer song (my favorite Weird Al song, actually) and is funny all the way through, catchy, and well-written. "Dare To Be Stupid" is another pastiche, parodying the style of Devo, but no specific song of theirs, and it's brilliant. I could go on, but for the most part I'd just be naming songs many people haven't heard of (but not you, I know *you* have, so before you go all nuclear hipster on me, I'll acknowledge beforehand that you, yes YOU in particular, have a mastery of this subject matter far and above that of the average layperson or myself, so please let it go...).

Watching Weird Al get all the acclaim he gets for rewriting the lyrics to songs other people made popular is like watching a master class painter get famous for doing paint-by-number velvet Elvises but adding KISS make-up or Hitler mustaches or googly-eyes to them. Funny? Yes, sometimes. Interesting? Yes, sometimes. Genius? Not so much...

I like Weird Al's original stuff a lot, and I do believe he has works of genius. I'm just disheartened by the thought that, as talented as he is, if he hadn't piggybacked off everyone else's material, he wouldn't be enjoying the degree of success he does today. And that is true of every parodist, regardless of who they are or how good they are. And I worry about what that means for me as a writer and performer.

But here's the kicker: I *like* parodies. I *love* them. I like writing them and singing them and singing along with them. But the song-writer in me who wants to be *worthy* of admiration finds them lacking. I watch some geek artists making entire careers out of parodies and think *that's just too easy.* And I've long said that I could be one of them if I could bring myself to do it, but...I can't. It's snobbish and I'm a jerk for it, but I don't want to be a parodist, not without being a songwriter first, and I just do not see them as the same thing, or even necessarily as equals. Mess up the words to a song you're singing, and you've created an accidental parody. I've yet to hear a song worth listening to that was created entirely by accident.

I know that parodies aren't worthless, but the artist in me who crafts both songs and parodies understands that parodies require less effort and are therefore, in my mental calculation at least, literally worth less. Not worthless, but *worth less*. You see? I know "The Star Spangled Banner" is a reworking of words to the tune of the popular English drinking song "Anacreon in Heaven." I know that there is a long and honored tradition of reworking words to previous tunes in various social and historical contexts.

I wish I could just let go and enjoy them, and I'm working on it. I really am. But a songwriter is a songwriter and a parodist is a parodist. A song is a song and a parody is a parody. And until my brain is less of an obsessive, pedantic asshole to me, that's just the way I'll have to reckon it. Like I said, I have a complicated relationship with parodies.

Summer of '83

I got my first d20
    Came in Red Box D&D
    Colored numbers in with a crayon
    It was summer of '83

Me, my brother & this kid named Terry
    Had a game in our front yard
    7th grade, Terry found girls and
    Left the game when his weenie got hard

Oh when I look back now
    That summer seemed to last forever
    And if I had the choice
    Hell Yeah - I'd always wanna be there
    Those were the best games of my life...

Well that didn't stop me from gaming,
    Kept it up through high school.
    Spent my evenin's behind a GM screen
    slingin' dice and drinkin' Mountain Dew, yeah!

Hanging out and slaying orcs!
    Boss fights that seemed to last forever...
    Oh, and in those dungeon crawls
    Killing wandering mobs for treasure!
    Those were the best games that I'd seen...
    Thanks to the summer of 83'

Man, then college came
    We were young and frustrated
    We needed to get laid...
    I guess nothin' can last forever...

And now the times are changin'
    A lot of gaming friends have come and gone
    Sometimes, behind my GM screen
    I look at LARP and wonder what went wrong

Hanging out and slaying orcs...
    Waiting for some guy to roll for treasure...
    Oh, and I still dungeon crawl...
    But my games these days are so much better...
    These are the best games that I'll see...
    Thanks to the Summer of 83'
    (Oh yeah) And Red Box D&D...

6

SUMMER OF '83

Obviously, "Summer of '83" is a parody of Bryan Adams' "Summer of '69," and I decided to write the parody in August or early September of 2011. *Impotent Nerd Rage* was released in August of 2011, and this wasn't written before tracking for that album was done, but I wanted to pad out the funny side of my geek set. This song made its live debut at the White Rabbit Cabaret in Fountain Square in Indianapolis on September 15 of 2011, and I recorded that show (both audio and video). I released the video on YouTube and the 'live single' on Bandcamp the next day.

I recorded a home studio version of it and posted that on Bandcamp as well, as soon as I determined that I'd never put it on an album. I'm not thrilled with the way that version of it came out, but I might be willing to give it another shot. I have a deep and abiding love for this parody... Again, I don't hate parodies, I just see them as innately requiring much, much less work, from an artist, less art, if you will, on the songwriting side.

This song takes me back to the days of playing D&D on the uncovered slab porch of our old trailer home in Greenwood, Indiana, in the blistering summer sun, feeling the excitement that only comes with discovery. We were discovering new worlds, new ways to be ourselves, and in no small way, who we were as people. I can't downplay that, even if this is a nostalgia-driven, comedic parody.

Lately I've been thinking about that summer a LOT. Playing *Dungeons & Dragons* wasn't all we did, of course. Every time I walk out my front door to check the mail or mow the lawn or just to step out for some air, and I'm greeted by a summer sun and a concrete porch, I end up flooded with memories of that summer and the summer after.

We didn't have air conditioning—or even a color TV yet, for that matter—and it was much cooler outside, at least when there was a breeze, than inside. My brother Neal and I, and sometimes one of our friends, Terry or Dave, would put cheap folding tray tables and kitchen chairs on the porch, and sit out in the sun and create. We'd draw comic characters, superheroes, and fantasy races or characters from the game, and write monster or character bios for the game. Neal was writing a science fiction novel about a character named John Faser that he called *Battle Beyond the Stars* (I'm not sure if he was consciously ripping off the title of the TV movie by the same name starring that guy from the Waltons or not, but we were kids). He had chapters and chapters of hand-written, 8th grade science fiction action, and I devoured it, when he'd let me.

There was something freeing about sitting on that porch, listening to WZPL ("Don't Pay The Ferryman" got cranked and sang along to every time it came on, which happened at least twice a day), and making things with our minds, designing and building intellectual real estate that would color our lives forever, some to greater degrees than others. It was formative. It was foundational. It was magical.

It was surprisingly disciplined for three middle-school kids.

And then there were the games... Being an elf and a wizard, a fighter and a dwarf. Nobody wanted to play a cleric or a thief early on. Slaying lizard-men and orcs, kobolds and goblins, casting spells and dividing treasure. Being heroes, saving villages and towns, rescuing captured townsfolk. I've made no secret that my gaming life, which influenced most aspects of my home and professional lives to a profound extent, began in that prepubescent summer sun.

There was a sense of wonder and discovery in the game. Every monster was new, held unforeseen dangers. Every spell, every stroke of a sword or axe was a kind of power we'd never experienced in games before. This was more than foundational, more than formative. This was transformative. This inspired us to create more, to do more, to be more, to find more magic. I sometimes joke onstage that my mom hated *Dungeons & Dragons*, but that couldn't be farther from the truth. She *knew* it wasn't evil, or maybe better yet, didn't care if it was. What she knew is that her kids could've been running around, doing drugs, causing problems, getting into trouble in the many, highly specialized ways that only seem like viable options for trailer park kids, but instead we were seated around a table all night, drinking sweet tea, reading books, telling each other stories in which we were the heroes doing heroic deeds, and doing math. My mom was a D&D fan.

The games also influenced what we would seek to create on that slab porch when we weren't gaming. Everything had already been centered around characters and stories, but now we were beginning to wonder what it would be like to build a medieval-style city, a theme park of sorts, and walk around in it, costumed, interacting as our characters. We were talking about LARPing (Live Action Role Playing) though we didn't know that term at the time, weren't aware of it at all. We simply saw it as a natural extension of what we were already doing, what we already wanted.

There were woods at the end of the court we lived on, and they were full of trails that we would play along. Over the years we built forts in the woods, went camping, and did our share of fantasizing about being our characters, but never as much as when we decided we wanted to figure out how to buy the land on which they stood and build that medieval settlement in them. We found large sheets of graph paper and began to design the city. We would call it Dragonfire and referred to the entire thought experiment (though at the time, we felt as if it were something a group of middle schoolers could somehow accomplish) *Project Dragonfire*. We had no doubt that if we wanted it bad enough and worked hard enough that it would happen. We never doubted each other's creative impulses that way.

Of course, it never happened. Middle turned to high school, and though we never stopped playing role-playing games, other diversions filled our minds, from girls to bands to cars and beyond. Adolescence does that to you, shifts your focus and attention without you even noticing it happening. Decades later, long after that sense of wonder and discovery has worn off, most of us still love role playing games, even if some of us don't play much (or at all) anymore. Some of us, though, took the opportunity to pass that wonder on to our kids, and to experience that wonder secondhand through their eyes.

When our oldest, Ben, was ten years old, I introduced him and his friends, Charles and Larken, to *Basic Dungeons & Dragons*—Red Box D&D, if you will. We started with the legendary *Keep On The Borderlands* module, my personal favorite for many reasons, and they had their first dispute when one of them wanted to kill all the kobolds in the Caves of Chaos, including the babies. It led to a surprisingly mature discussion, one that my gaming groups likely wouldn't have had as middle-schoolers, and some group decision making, and maybe only one or two thinly veiled threats. Just kidding. They weren't veiled at all.

But I kept gaming with my kids and their friends. At 9 years old, our youngest, Jack, experienced his first character death when an earth elemental attacked his dwarven monk with a critical hit and then rolled maximum damage. He went down to -61 hit points, and for a moment we thought it would be okay, but then the tears started flowing. Mama saved the day with freshly made cake whilst I quickly conferred with the other boys in the group, and they agreed that it was okay if I changed the magic item they would have gotten for a scroll of True Resurrection. Ben's paladin recovered an ear of the dwarf from the wall, and they soon were happy dungeon delvers once more. Plus, there was cake.

Another time, Charles, playing a wizard, frustrated by Ben's insistence on wanting a magic staff that was unquestionably a better fit for the wizard than the paladin, stormed off from the table calling the paladin a "sword-wielding, sword-wielding monkey," (and yes, he actually said "sword-wielding" twice. He was in his early teens and admirably kept himself from cursing, table-flipping, or dice-throwing. I was so proud of him). We still use that insult in personal conversations to this day.

Now all but Jack are grown. Charles runs games for his circle of friends. Ben has served for years in the Navy and has his own gaming groups and gaming group frustrations. Our youngest is in high school, and I don't know how much longer he'll be gaming with me (or at a table top for that matter. He seems to prefer computer-based games, though he plays in multiple roleplaying games, both online and in person).

I continue to play, with my regular gaming group and with pickup groups, at home, online, on the road, or at conventions, happy to have shown my children and their friends and even some of my adult friends how it's possible to make some of your happiest memories out of events that never really happened in places that don't exist anywhere outside of our minds. If that's not magic, nothing is. I still try to surround myself with friends who support my wild creative ideas, indulge my flights of creative fancy, and who have similar impulses to create and make and do things that I can support. There is a magic in that, as well. It's the magic of having a social support group, the magic of encouragement without ridicule, the magic of finding your tribe. And few things can be better for you, creatively, than that.

This parody somehow seems to recapture that feeling and provides an in-road for audiences at conventions and casual audiences as well. Not only do a lot of audience members relate to the lyrics, but even those that don't almost all know the song "Summer of '69," which provides a different repeatability, a different instant sense of familiarity and intimacy with my performance. It's a very mercenary and utilitarian viewpoint, but I've mentioned my complicated relationship with parodies, so maybe it's a necessary view. When I do write them, I often impose additional restrictions on myself when doing so, to make them harder, but I had no such conscious compunc-tion here. Looking back on it, though, every word of it is true, and that's a restriction in and of itself. There's no embellishment for artistic effect, it's just what happened. Which is kind of cool, I guess. Nerd cool. Geek cool. As cool as I get, at least.

It was the best game ever... The traps and riddles were so clever,
　　And hardly any of our party even died
　　Except for George, but he deserved it. He kept doing really dumb
shit.
　　We split his magic items up, I swear to God he almost cried.

And when he came back in the game with his new gnome thief mage
assassin
　　We stole all his gear again and sold him as a slave.

This was the best game ever! I took his set of +4 leather
　　Then we hopped aboard the plot train, let it take us for a ride,
　　But then George came back...And this time he was a druid
　　Who refused to leave the forest and always tried to start a fight.

And that's exactly what he did with a poor farmer on the outskirts
　　Of the town who turned out to be a god in disguise.

Best. Game. Ever. 'Cause George's druid's head got severed
　　And he came back in the game while we were going through
this cave
　　To slay a dragon. This time he was a barbarian,
　　Who hated both our magic users, but had a magic sword of flame.
　　And when we reached the dragon's lair he argued tactics for an
hour,
　　Til we fed him to the dragon and then killed it in three rounds.

BEST. GAME. EVER.

And as we wound down the adventure, back in town inside the
tavern,
　　George was there as a half elf/half orcish monk illusionist.

And as we counted out our treasure he insisted on attempting
To seduce the barmaid, laughing as she cried and raised her fists.

Until he saw all of our weapons raised, and as he died he swore
That he would never game with us again as long as he lived.

BEST! GAME! EVER! Saved a barmaid, slayed a dragon,
Got the treasure, raised a flagon, And we racked up the XP.
And we will never have to deal with George's bullshit
In another game again, that is at least until next week.

Cause he is the GM's brother, and his mom won't let us game there
In her basement anymore, unless we say that he can play.
And I know you had to be there, but I swear to all that's holy,
Victory was never sweeter than it was today.

Best Game Ever...

7

BEST GAME EVER

In August of 2011 Neil Gaiman retweeted a YouTube video by Allie Goertz called "Tonight (A D&D Song)", and I watched the video because one of my favorite authors thought it was worth sharing and because it was about something I'm very, very interested in. Her song was sweet and charming and wistful, and romanticized the notion of *Dungeons & Dragons* as beautiful escapism, and as I enjoyed the song, I realized that the vast majority of the games I played in growing up weren't so sweet. There was very little to be romanticized about the games of my youth, except through the lenses of nostalgia, and so I almost immediately began composing a response song titled "Best Game Ever."

I wrote the song at our dining room table in our big, blue farm-house in Redkey, Indiana, and the words just flowed. The video was shot and posted the same day. It happened fast, and I wrote the lyrics out by hand while I was writing the song (something I rarely do anymore) and had to have them taped up in front of me just off camera so that I could perform the song. I still have those hand-written lyrics somewhere.

My song, of course, focuses on a gaming group plagued by an attention-seeking player named George, who tends to derail every gaming session until it's entirely about him, and how that group responds by spending a day of gaming in which every time George's character begins to derail the game, they either kill the character or find another way to remove that character from the game. Of course, each time George creates a new character and returns, trying again to find a way to derail the adventure.

I'm often asked if George is based on a real person, and the answer is yes. George is based on many real people, myself being one of them. We've all gamed with a George once or twice, or maybe much more often, and we've all been George more often that we'd care to admit. Let's face it: if you're in a gaming group and can't immediately identify who the George is, it's more than likely *you*.

In my own gaming life, I've seen an elven character armed with a whip and a crossbow named Indiana Elf. Confession time: that was my character, and the other players were pretty blunt about how they couldn't wait until he died. They tormented poor Indiana Elf until I begged to be allowed to change characters, except my brother Neal, our DM, wouldn't let me kill him off arbitrarily or let me roll a new character, but finally relented and allowed me to play the character of Cobra, our fat, fighter hireling who was a full two levels lower than everyone else.

I've seen a low-level magic user named Merlin who agreed to worship a Mary Sue goddess named Aleena who was created by the DM (again, my brother Neal). Aleena only ever appeared nude and required all of her subjects to also remain completely nude, including armor, so no one in the party agreed to worship her except for Merlin, who wouldn't take a loss to his Armor Class for being naked because he wasn't allowed to wear armor anyway. In exchange for his obeisance, she granted Merlin the glaive from the 80's movie *Krull*. In high school, we agreed to play a homebrew campaign under a DM who told us he had created his own world, and halfway through his description of it, ten minutes into the first session, before we actually played anything, everyone recognized it as *The Legend of Zelda*. He didn't even change the name of the Tri-Force.

We once played a campaign with a paladin in the party who had just earned his mount (this was just after the release of *Unearthed Arcana*), and who talked Neal into allowing him to have a Griffon as a mount (he'd wanted a Dragonne and this was somehow the compromise). This was, of course, first edition AD&D, which meant that the paladin, played by a member of the gaming group who, by sheer coincidence, I assure you, was named George, was required to be of the Lawful Good alignment. In retrospect, it felt like Lawful Stupid. The rest of the players hated that paladin, and we were jealous of and hated his mount. When George had to miss a session and the Griffon died under mysterious and questionable circumstances, sacrificing itself for the good of the party, George left the gaming group for a while.

Here's an interesting story about that particular George (the real player, not the George from the song): When my mom died in 2015, she was buried in a cemetery not too far from the trailer park in which I spent my formative gaming years, so I had Jody drive Jack and I through and around the park, reminiscing about old times and old games. I'd been drinking and crying and was quite maudlin and emotional. I showed them the very spot, the cement slab porch where I rolled my first character, Tran the elf. It was Basic D&D, so elf was a class of its own. I'd just seen Tron at a library showing and I've already admitted my youthful predilection for borrowing names from popular media. My second character, rolled that same day on that same porch, was a magic-user named Thorin, because I was ten years old and didn't remember that the wizard in *The Hobbit* was named Gandalf, at least not until I had already written Thorin on my character sheet. Neal, a natural to the role of punishing arbitrator—err—Dungeon Master, refused to let me rename him.

I showed them the trailer in which we played our very first game, Neal, me, and Terry (yes—the Terry from "Summer of '83". I told you that song was 100% truthful). It was still there in the park thirty-two years later, blue and dilapidated, but in my mind I could see it exactly as it was that day. Our older sister had lived there, rented it, and we played that first session in one of the empty, unfurnished bedrooms, me with Tran and Thorin, and Terry with a fighter and a dwarf whose names I'll probably never remember. Our characters were walking a trail in the forest, and Neal would ask us how far we were traveling. It was new and weird, and we didn't say that we'd walk until the trail turned or forked, but rather that we'd walk ten feet, and then another twenty feet, and then another twenty feet, and so on, until he told us that we couldn't move that far because the trail turned. It felt, at the time, like a verbal game of *Zork*, until we were set upon by bandits.

"How do we know they're bandits?" I asked.

"Because they're trying to kill and rob you," Neal said.

So we fought and killed the bandits, which involved our first DM retcon, because one of our characters (I'm pretty sure it was Tran) died during the fight. As a player, the dice have always hated me. When I DM, the dice have usually hated the PCs playing. Go figure. But Neal decided that the game would suck if one of our characters died right off, so he left Tran alive after the bandits were defeated. That combat was magical, with us describing what we wanted our characters to do and Neal describing what the bandits did in response, and the dice deciding all our fates. It was glorious and new and other games would pale in comparison to me forever. Then our characters moved on, following the trail ten and twenty feet at a time, navigating curves and forks until Neal said, "That's it."

"What do you mean, that's it?"

"That's it," he said again. "We've run out of map. I only made the one."

And we sighed and packed up our stuff and went home, urging him to make more maps because we were addicted.

I showed them where we would enter the woods where we wanted to build *Project: Dragonfire*, and bemoaned that, instead of the magical wooded trails from my memories, it now led to the back fence of someone's yard in a subdivision. As we left the trailer park, I took them through the subdivision where George had lived.

I had Jody stop there. I leaned out the passenger window and took a picture of the front door on my phone, making sure not to have any identifying information in frame. The next day, after I'd sobered up, I posted the picture on Facebook with the (somewhat misleading) caption, "Took a trip down memory lane yesterday. This is the actual house George (the real Best Game Ever George) lived in."

There were many comments, including from Neal, who commented, "No shout outs to the DM of the best game ever? *cough cough*," and questions about whether he actually played a gnome thief-mage-assassin. I replied that I wasn't going to spoil the magic by dissecting the song any more than I already had, but suffice it to say that the song is filled with truth, even if it isn't entirely factual, and pointed out to be fair that George wasn't always the "George" in our group. We all took turns being the asshat. Someone asked if George knew about the song, and if he'd forgiven me. I replied that I hadn't spoken with George since the 80s and didn't even know if he was still alive (some of our friends from way back then sadly aren't).

I got distracted by real life, then, walked away and forgot about the posting for a couple of hours. While I was gone, however, another very old friend from that set of gaming groups, one who had attended Mom's funeral, saw my post and began to comment.

The thing about friends, especially very old friends who you don't see very often, is that they don't necessarily keep up with your career. Or maybe they do, but it's only peripherally, and they don't really understand that you have fans, now. Of course, you don't have fans, right? You were the kid who played Indiana Elf for Odin's sake. And even if they grasp that you have a few fans (I mean it couldn't be very many, right? I *know* this guy), perhaps they don't consider the inquisitive, enthusiastic, seeking nature of fandom and the lack of perceived boundaries that sometimes come with it.

It seems he'd went online, found George on Facebook, and posted a comment to the thread making clear in no uncertain terms that George was very much alive and that his profile was RIGHT HERE, linking George's profile in the comments. It was up for an hour or two before I discovered it and took it down. I don't remember how many times it had been liked or reacted to. I posted in the comments that I had deleted that comment, that I was glad George was found, but I didn't want him inundated with requests or other nonsense

because of my song, and I didn't want to give some of my more enthusiastic fans the chance.

I'm not sure it registered with him, or that he believed me, or that
he understood, but that's okay. We're still friends. As for George? I
don't know how many friend requests or questions he got during that
two-hour period. I don't know that anyone actually said anything to
him, or if he is even aware, to this very day, of my song in any way,
shape, or form. But I can and will confirm that he has yet to accept my
friend request.

It's okay. I've met me. I understand.

Han Solo Cool

Another crappy shift at work, a thankless job that's only perk
    is quitting time so I can get away from all these jerks and,
    I see you walk by every day, past my window on your way
    To somewhere better than this hell hole where I earn my pay but,

You don't notice me at all. I'm too afraid to take a fall.
    If I were someone else I'd say hi, but I stall.

If I could just be cool like Han Solo, if I could misbehave like Captain
Mal,
    If I could just be half as smooth as Lando, I could get a grip on life
somehow.
    Life would simply rule, if I could be Han Solo cool.

My manager thinks that I'm nuts, I finally work up the guts,
    To ask you out. I step outside, he follows me, we see you but, BUT
    My parking meter's out of time, I left all of my change inside,
    He's got a date, I've got a ticket by the time I've grabbed a dime.

This doesn't seem too fair at all, I'm hurt and sickened by his gall,
    I'd quit my job and kick his ass if I had balls...

If I could just be cool like Han Solo, if I could misbehave like Captain
Mal,
    If I could just be half as smooth as Lando, I could get a grip on life
somehow.
    If I could kick some Alien ass like Ripley, if I could make you laugh
like Dr. Who,
    If I could follow treasure maps like Indy, they would always lead
me back to you.
    Life would simply rule, if I could be Han Solo cool.

If I were thawed from carbonite would you let me hold you tight?

If I were a scoundrel could I steal your heart and steal a kiss goodnight?

If I could just learn to shoot first instead of waiting for the worst,

I'd Kessel run for you blindfolded in reverse...

Punch it, Chewie!

If I could just be cool like Han Solo, if I could misbehave like Captain Mal,

If I could just be half as smooth as Lando, I could get a grip on life somehow.

If I could kick some Alien ass like Ripley, if I could make you laugh like Dr. Who,

If I could follow treasure maps like Indy, they would always lead me back to you.

Life would simply rule, if I could be Han Solo cool...

If I could be Han Solo...

You'd say, "I love you." I'd say, "I know."

8

HAN SOLO COOL

I used to introduce "Han Solo Cool" the same way every time onstage. It was a holdover of being a musical standup comic. There were certain "bits" I'd go into that would lead into a song, set it up, and then I'd carry the thread to the next song after with the next bit, create transitions, make it seamless. Most audiences weren't really used to that from a standup comic. They were used to a comic who played guitar either just playing funny songs the whole time or doing a standup portion and then picking up their guitar to play for the last half. I did both, interweaved throughout, and it made my shows a lot more like a funny episode of MTV Unplugged. It made them accessible and made them make sense, have a sense of continuity throughout.

Before "Han Solo Cool," I would—and still sometimes do—talk about how being an artist was a sort of curse upon your family, because you create from what you know and what you know is, in large part, your family, so you, by necessity, draw considerable artistic inspiration from them. I'd talk about how one of the most common phrases spoken in our household would come after an argument or disagreement, when things got heated and we'd backed off to different areas of the house for space, and then I'd hear Jody shout from the other side of the house, "And don't you dare write a song about that!"

It wouldn't matter, though. By that time, I was halfway to writing the bridge.

In one of my favorite movies, *That Thing You Do!*, (and here's a spoiler warning if you still haven't seen it and want to watch it unsullied by previous information) Liv Tyler's character Faye tells Jimmy, "Shame on me for kissing you with my eyes closed so tight." That entire speech, leading up to that line, every time I watch it, I spend thinking, *Oh, yeah. He's storing every word away for a song*, because I damn sure would've been. It's a fantastic line and a great speech, and he'd be guaranteed a good song would come from it. But back to the intro to "Han Solo Cool"...

I'd talk about "don't you dare write a song about that," and then I'd talk about how sometimes something happened, someone said something or you just happened upon a combination of words or whatever and you KNEW you were going to use it, creatively. Call it found art or lightning striking or instant inspiration or whatever. It is genuinely what happened in this instance.

Jack was young, only 8 years old, and had just watched *Star Wars* for the first time. A younger person would probably clarify that statement by saying *Episode IV* or *A New Hope*, or both, but that feels awkward to me because growing up (and hell, even after it was out on video and got the "official" subtitle,) it was still just *Star Wars* to us. Anyway, Jack had just seen the first *Star Wars* movie, the original theatrical release (because when *Star Wars* was first released on DVD the theatrical release was the bonus disc, and being the purist geek snob that I am, it's what I put in the player for him).

When the movie was done, he said, "Dad, I wish I was as cool as Han Solo," and boom. I knew right then I was going to write that song. It was a matter of when, not if.

I was working on material for my second album, which I already decided would be titled *Barbarian Jetpack*, and just knew "Han Solo Cool" would be on that album. Writing the song was an exercise in storytelling in the verse and creating a chorus with a broader appeal and a good hook. I can't go too much into it, because there's not much to tell. I just...wrote it. Like many geeks, I'd had a lot of experience with rejection, feeling like I don't fit in, and with being hesitant to take chances or ask someone out because of personal insecurities. I thought about the heroes from TV and film who behave the way we want to be, those idols who seem to be either completely above insecurity or able to do awesome things despite such feelings. I strung together a story about an insecure someone in a mundane situation who wants to feel cool, like those heroes.

I've been told by some fans that I should never do a live show without playing that song, and they might be right, but that's something that gets harder to do the more I write and record. I've released more than 100 songs and have more unreleased songs than that, and keeping any one song as a permanent inclusion to a set list is hard. "She Don't Like Firefly" and "Best Game Ever" aren't always on my set list, and they're arguably my best-known songs.

Here's a final, quick but amusing story about the song: I often perform at DragonCon, which is ostensibly the "largest multi-media, pop culture convention focusing on science fiction & fantasy, gaming, comics, literature, art, music, and film in the universe," but might just be an extended Labor Day weekend full of alcohol-fueled, cosplay-themed debauchery. I'm not saying that like it's a bad thing, mind you. One year, I had an audience member from Australia purchase my albums after a show, something which is always an awesome feeling, no matter how many times it happens. A year passed, another Drag-onCon came around, and we both found ourselves there again. After one of my shows, they said they had some questions about one of my lyrics they didn't quite understand.

"Why would you want to follow treasure maps like Ghandi?" they asked. The way I sing the line, between my midwest American accent and their Australian accent, they weren't clear as to whom I was alluding, and they'd interpreted the name in the line as Ghandi. I explained that the lyric was Indy, as in Indiana Jones, not Ghandi, and we both laughed.

They said, "That makes so much more sense!"

But now, every time I sing the line, and I mean every time, I see Mahatma Ghandi in a fedora with a bullwhip in my mind's eye. I smile about it—who wouldn't?—and I have to fight from singing "follow treasure maps like Ghandi." Little moments like that fill songs with new life and, as Marie Kondo would say, spark joy.

"Han Solo Cool" is framed around the story of an awkward guy trying to get the girl, which is something a lot of us can identify with. Still, even though I'm not in any sense as cool as Han Solo, sometimes I feel like I have my moments. Now, I am not a distinctly handsome man and I'm thicker around the middle than I used to be. I accept this. I had my charms when I was younger, a baby-faced, good-looking kid, back when I had a waist and a hairline, but I wouldn't say I've ever been strikingly attractive and never had droves of potential partners blatantly hitting on me.

It does happen on occasion, though, which serves to remind me that I'm not wholly unattractive and that's a good thing, feeling attractive. If it does happen on a regular basis, maybe I'm just dense enough that I don't recognize it. Let's face it. I'm pretty insecure, and telling myself that someone isn't interested in me in any sense, let alone a romantic one, is the easy-button default setting of my soul. In any case, here are three times I knew—KNEW—unequivocally, that someone was hitting on me while I was on the road.

The last time I remember it happening was in Fort Walton Beach, Florida, at a venue called The Block. It was September 22, 2016 (I looked it up... I have the dates of all my bookings recorded, but it's not like I remember these things off the top of my head), and The Block was one of those venues that had multiple clubs in one. There was a pool room/bar with a small stage, where the comedy was, a cowboy/country bar with a mechanical bull and a larger stage, some other bar, and a karaoke bar.

It was in the karaoke bar, after the show, that I was approached. She hadn't been at the comedy show, and I can't remember who she was or what she said, but she was interested enough that I noticed. Sat down at my table, where I was sitting alone when not singing, despite there being other tables, other seats available, and started flirting with me between songs. I remember leaving before I'd sung the last couple of songs I had in because I didn't want to set any sort of expectations, and she was getting starting to get DRUNK—she seemed to have had a head start on it when she got to the bar. Anyway, I called Jody and left, driving back to the hotel.

In March of 2011 in Port Orange, FL, at a club called Trappuzzano's, I was approached by an attractive woman after the show while I was selling merch (merchandise) outside the club. I'd sell CDs, of course, and sometimes bumper stickers, but most of my merch money came from t-shirt sales. I sold 2 different t-shirts, each related to a different part of my act. One read, "It's A Licky-Licky Night" and the other was an ambigram, a design that read differently when you looked at it upside down. Right-side up, that shirt read, "Yes Dear," but upside down it read, "Fuck You." I was outside because they'd begun to play dance music as soon as the comedy show had finished, and I just wasn't into it. I remember her talking with me about my act a little bit and how she enjoyed it, then said, "You mention your wife in your act. Just how married are you?"

"I'm *that* married," I responded.

"That's too bad," she said, then bought an "It's A Licky-Licky Night" t-shirt and walked away.

The most memorable time, though, was one of the first times it ever happened to me on the road. I was in Fort Walton Beach, Florida (yep, apparently, that's a great location for me), but this was years before, at the original Comedy Zone location there, a dueling piano bar called Howl at the Moon. The comedy would happen between sets of the dueling piano guys. They'd finish their set, act as the emcee and introduce the feature act (the "middle" act), and the feature would introduce the headliner (or closer). I was the feature and it was my first time there.

This had the reputation of being an unusually tough room for comics to play, as the business model of Howl at the Moon is to get a room full of drunk, loud people screaming songs at each other. They loved me, though, and by the end of my set I had the 2-300 people in the room all singing the Muppet Babies theme song. After the show, I was at the bar tipping the bar staff for taking care of me when a very pretty young woman (young enough to get carded in the bar) asked if she could buy me a drink. Now, the comics drank for free, but I said yes and the bartenders loved me for it because they could charge her the cost of my drink, not ring it up, and take the extra as a tip. So I let her buy me a shot of Jim Beam and she introduced herself to me.

She said, and I'm not kidding, "I'm Jenny, but my Native American name is Gonna Get Laid Tonight."

I smiled, drained the glass, and shot back, "I'm Mikey, and my Native American name is Jerks Off Alone In Hotel Room."

She gave me a funny look, and at that exact moment, my cell phone rang. It was Jody. I looked at it and said, "It's my wife. It's like she knew you just bought me a drink or something."

Then I answered the call without missing a beat and said, "It's like you felt a disturbance in the force." By the time I got off the phone, I was in my car, headed back to the hotel room, and Jenny was probably out there making someone's night. You're welcome, random unknown person.

You're welcome.

Scoobythulhu

I'd had enough of rubber masks, and holograms, of flash bombs and machine-made fog.

I'd had enough of those meddling kids, and their stupid, talking dog.

I found my deliverance in the prison library, hidden in an ancient tome.

I found the words that would grant my vengeance, rouse the old ones from their home...

It all began when their hippie van broke down in Massachusetts, in a sudden summer
    storm.

Near a quaint old town, there was shelter found in a haunted bed and breakfast, a place to
    dry off and get warm.

The stoner and his coward dog said, "We don't want to get involved!"

But the other three, in their deviant glee, "Said there's a mystery to be solved!"

And I knew they were mine!

I swore that I would crush you, that I would kill you, Scooby Doo!

I swore that I would break you, so now I turn to... Cthulhu!

A secret passage found with no one around and suddenly Daphne's missing, to no one's
    real surprise.

She soon returned all bruised and burned from fierce tentacular groping all up and down
    her thighs.

She said the passage led her dark and alone to a secret place near the millionaire's home,

But the second before the gang left to explore, they were joined by Davy Jones.

Friggin' Monkee, Davy Jones!

I swore that I would crush you, that I would kill you, Scooby Doo!
    I swore that I would break you, so now I turn to... Cthulhu!

Velma's glasses broke and while Davy Jones helped her crawl around to find them, a
    mirror suddenly turned to black.
    Shaggy's glance was drawn through the mirror beyond to the void home of Yog-Sothoth,
    and his sanity quickly cracked.
    As Shag and Scoob tried to run away, brave Fred rushed in to save the day,
    And when Daphne, possessed, moved to kill and molest him, Velma stabbed her in the
    chest
    With a pitchfork no less!

I swore that I would crush you, that I would kill you, Scooby Doo!
    I swore that I would break you, so now I turn to... Cthulhu!

Long story short, turns out the owners of the old hotel... Well, that was me, and I'd
    created this whole scenario to lure the Mystery Inc gang into my grasp.
    And sure, they managed to stop the great Cthulhu from leaving his slumbering depths
    under the waves. And I went back to prison, silently awaiting the return of my master to
    devour my unworthy soul.
    And Shaggy was mostly okay—after some extensive counseling. Of course this only

happened after Scooby lost a leg in one of their late night food orgies. Turns out Shaggy

had a taste for dog meat. They don't talk anymore.

Even Daphne made it out alive—though it looked like she was a goner. That cursed Davy

Jones ran into a peculiar text while looking for Velma's glasses, damn his silky smooth

voice and dreamy good looks.

The book showed her how to revive the dead by reducing them to their vital essences and

reconstructing them through ritual magic. This involved Velma flaying Daphne while she

was still barely alive and wearing her skin like a flesh mask. She's institutionalized now.

Davy used to visit her once in a while, but it got too depressing.

Fred is still plucking away at mysteries with Daphne, too oblivious to realize that no one

was wearing a rubber mask, and stupid enough to believe the child in her womb is

actually his.

That's an episode of Maury I can't wait for. Wait'll he sees the tentacles...

Muahahahahhahahahah!

I swore that I would break you, I gave my soul to Cthulhu...

I swore that I would crush you, that I would kill you, Scooby Doo!

9

SCOOBYTHULHU

In late February of 2011, I sent an email to Dr. Bob Arens, a game developer/designer, role-playing game enthusiast, possessor of multiple degrees, and a fellow fan of the Fear the Boot podcast. I asked if he'd write me a recap of the events from a game he'd run at Fear The Con III the year before, in 2010, where the players took on the roles of the Scooby gang and special guest stars, like they had in *The New Scooby Doo Movies* from 1972-74. Full disclosure: I didn't play in that game, which is why I asked for a recap of the game session.

I was scheduled to play in the sequel game in 2011, where I would guest star as myself, comedian Mikey Mason. During *that* game, Velma (played by Stacey Rigger) referred to me consistently and repeatedly as "Mediocre Comedian Mikey Mason," which I found hilarious and is still an in-joke with the group from that game to this day. For a short time, I considered using it as official branding for my act, but ultimately decided against it for what should be obvious reasons. In any case, I sent that email for the express purpose of writing a song based on that first, older game session, because I'd heard the stories recounted from several of the players and observers and even people playing at adjacent tables, and thought it was too good to pass up.

I'd been appearing at Fear The Con since their second convention in 2009, but had been performing my regular stage act, and now was harboring aspirations of doing a geek album, a geek act. I already had ideas for some songs, though. I was writing a song called "She Don't Like Firefly," and I had vague ideas for songs called "Too Fat To Troop" and "Me and Alan Moore's Beard," pretty concrete ideas about a tune I wanted to call "Kobolds Ate My Baby," and I thought it would be fun, and maybe even easy, to write a song about Bob's Scooby-Thulhu game. I was a bit shortsighted. Having a plot and following the plot in verse, with a chorus and a hook, are very different things.

Bob's emailed response was quick and thorough, beginning with "Ho-kay... where to start..." and ending 7 hefty paragraphs later with, "Anyhow. If you want any more detail on any of this, just let me know. Hope this wasn't too long." I thanked him and set to work...on "She Don't Like Firefly," which I wrote and re-wrote and finally recorded and released on YouTube in early March of 2011, just before Fear The Con IV. It went viral as I was attending the convention, and that song was performed live at FTC4, but I've told that story before.

As I said, I played myself in the sequel to ScoobyThulhu, where Don Knotts and I helped the Scooby Gang unravel the mystery of the G-G-G-Ghost Shark! I ran my first game at a convention, that year (Ghostbusters, by West End Games), had a great time, and drove home, excited to begin work on an album.

I got home and got to work on the Kickstarter for *Impotent Nerd Rage*, and when it funded, got to work on the album. "ScoobyThulhu" obviously didn't make it to that first album, in fact I didn't even get around to writing it until November of 2012. I started with the idea that it should be an 80s metal song with a long, spooky intro. I worked on it while recording the demo up in my "secret lair," my upstairs office at our home in Redkey, Indiana, writing the verses and adding them in to the demo. There was a lot to adapt, even as sparing as I was using the given plot points. I realized after a couple hours of work that I would have to cut the Harlem Globetrotters and all of their subplots, as well as any non-essential characters, else I'd have a song to rival Iron Butterfly's "In-A-Gadda-Da-Vida" in length. I worked and made cuts, reworked and made more cuts, and still, 5 minutes or so into the song, I ended up going into summary mode, using the words "Long story short..."

That's correct. Five minutes and sixteen seconds into a seven minute and nine second song, I spend the rest of the song summing up with almost two minutes of narration over a musical overture. I knew "ScoobyThulhu" would never be marketable by any normal standard. I only hoped that my fellow geeks would like it enough to forgive the length.

Scott Lindell, my freshman roommate in college and a member of my weekly gaming group, played lead guitar on the song, and the bass was Jason Tompkins. I recorded each of their parts at their respective homes on my laptop and mixed it at my own home.

I finished recording and mixing the song and sent a copy via email to Bob on November 6, 2012, with the following note: "I had to eliminate the Globetrotters from the story altogether, and everything else ended up a little truncated, and I still ended up with a seven minute song. Please remember that even though this is the final, mastered version, and even though you are perfectly permitted to talk about it if you'd like--even on social media--I haven't released it for public consumption quite yet. I hope you like it, as you certainly inspired it."

In fact, he did more than inspire it. His synopsis informed the way I wrote the song itself. The opening lines of the song, once the story proper begins, very much reflect the way in which he wrote his recap. His first few sentences were:

"It all began when the Mystery Machine broke down in upstate Massachusetts. The Scooby Gang had to find refuge from the sudden storm at a nearby bed and breakfast, run by a kindly old couple who had also taken in Davy Jones of the Monkees, and the Harlem Globetrotters, whose sports car and tour bus (respectively) had broken down. The couple told their visitors that they were happy to provide shelter, but it was too bad that nasty ol' Mr. Dashville, a local millionaire, was trying to buy their place. Looks like he would be able to, too

- not many folks had wanted to stay there since the stories about the old witch that haunted the place had gotten started!"

It's not difficult to see where I drew inspiration and tone from his storytelling.

"ScoobyThulhu" is one of those songs that has a ton of words and can be hard to perform live. I use a simplified version of the chords rather than attempting to play and sing it the way it was actually written and recorded, and I have to have the lyrics in front of me or the "long story short" from the end becomes a jumbled, longer mess instead of a more succinct summary of events. But it's also one of those songs that people tend to like more than I ever suspected they would. It's not unusual for someone to request it at a show, or for someone to get excited on the increasingly rare occasions when I do play it at conventions, since it's a seven-minute song, which means it'll take up almost two songs worth of time from my usual hour-long sets, and require me to go over the song at least in passing before I perform it. During online shows, it's much less of an imposition, but still not a frequent visitor to my set list.

Barbarian Jetpack was released on November 15, 2012. with the title to the track, to my chagrin, misspelled on the album. The final "H" before the final "U" was left out on the album art and track title of the digital master file, and it's one of those things I've made marginal but continual attempts to correct ever since. In September, 2014, I cobbled together a video using clips of Scooby Doo episodes and a Lovecraft-inspired episode of *The Real Ghostbusters*. You can find that on YouTube, with "ScoobyThulhu" spelled correctly. Watch it, enjoy it, share it.

Just please don't request it at a show.

Mad

Hello Daily Journal, connect me to Tom Evander
    He wrote the piece today on Dr. Romulus.
    I was both anxious and offended, and because I am said Doctor,
    Find the claim that I am evil more than slightly libelous.

I don't really want to rule world, but it's done such a horrid job
    Of ruling itself, maybe it's my time.
    On the other hand I ache for the eternal void of chaos
    Its a bifurcated world view, but it's mine.

In the meantime, it's best if you desist.
    I can't let you call me evil, I simply must insist...

I'm not evil, I'm insane and slightly angry,
    A more accurate descriptor would be mad.
    So kindly check your rhetoric, your demagogic verbiage.
    To draw my full attentions would be bad.
    Because I'm mad!

Wake up, Tom, I know it's late and it is likely quite unsettling
    For me to turn up armed and at your home.
    Please ignore the robots, they're just for my protection,
    They react to sudden movements, so it's best if you stay prone.

I think we both want what is best, ending hunger and unrest,
    But we share differing ideologies.
    Though our methods demarcate us, all that really separates us is
    A hundred IQ points and maybe sociopathy.

I'm not evil, I'm insane and pretty angry,
    A more accurate descriptor would be mad.
    So kindly check your rhetoric, your demagogic verbiage.

MIKEY MASON

To draw my full attentions would be bad.
Because I'm mad!

Perhaps you think I'm evil for the things that I have done, but I just don't have the time or
    will to justify each one.
    I'm a man of many masters, and I live a paradox: Bending the world to my new order, just
    as I incite chaos.

Now, Tom, I'm very angered, in your article today,
    You called me evil in at least a dozen different ways.
    In the first sentence alone you used the words loathsome and base,
    Malignant and malicious, heinous, vile and depraved.

Well your thesaurus surely warranted it's cover price today,
    and that brings us to our business here tonight.
    Because of your transgressions, you'll be torn apart by robots,
    But if it's any consolation, it turns out that you were right!

I may be evil, but I'm still insanely angry,
    And that only reinforces that I'm mad!
    And you had to shoot your mouth off, be the real voice of the people,
    And you drew my full attention and that's bad...

Because I'm mad...
    Evil and mad.

10

MAD

"Mad" was written in 2013 during the songwriting process for the *Dangerous Gifts* album (although I don't remember if I'd selected the name of the album yet or not.) At the time I was still in full swing as a stand-up comic, and quite sensitive to the fact that people thought my songs were sort of... anti-intellectual. The reality is, despite the content of those songs, there was still a level of craftsmanship to them that's hard to fake, especially in the word-smithing. A couple of those songs got about as obscene as a person could get without ever using a single curse word.

I was writing at the time to be "radio dirty," meaning that you couldn't use curse words, but innuendo was fine. It almost didn't matter, because Justin Timberlake and Janet Jackson had killed most of that nearly a decade before with the "wardrobe malfunction" at the 2004 Super Bowl. Radio stations were the hardest hit by the FCC fines after that, because people would be flipping through their stations, hear something that offended them, and report it to the FCC —something that somehow just didn't happen with TV. This is at least partially because people don't stay on a TV station long enough to see or hear something they consider offensive if they're just flipping channels, but using the SCAN feature on a car radio leaves you on each station for a few seconds, long enough for you to hear something (either in or, more likely, out of context) and become righteously indignant about it. And by you, I don't mean you specifically, but rather the type of people who would call the FCC and report a radio station because of innuendo.

Also, TV networks tend to both have and make much more money than radio, and spend it on both lawyers and self-censors. Soon after the nipple-slip-seen-round-the-world, radio stations "cleaned up" their content out of necessity, though it has loosened back up a bit, a trend that will likely continue until the Next Greatly Offensive Thing To Happen™, whatever that is. But I digress.

Although it takes a great facility with language to write a clever, dirty song that doesn't use dirty words, or to piece together some of the metaphors that I used in my standup comedy music, or even more specifically to give a strong, funny metaphor that both rhymes and scans, all while writing a full, original, catchy tune... the real art and craft of the writing got obscured by the fact that the songs were funny and *seemed* like they were easy to write (because that's what good craftsmanship looks like. Like it's just easy).

As a reaction, I was determined to write a song that both used that level of craftsmanship and showcased my vocal range and my vocabulary. That turned out to be "Mad." I have distinct memories of writing it at the dining room table at our home in Redkey.

I chose the newspaper name *Daily Journal* because it was the name of the newspaper in Franklin, IN, where I went to elementary and high school—my middle school years were spent in Greenwood, IN, at Center Grove Middle School, if you must know. Tom Evander was chosen because I wanted a strong, monosyllabic first name followed by a three-syllable last name, for scansion and meter purposes, and I wanted the name to subtly evoke the concept of an evangelist, as I intended the character to be an evangelist of truth, and to rail against Dr. Romulus with great passion in his writings as part of the backstory of the song. Evander worked perfectly in that capacity.

The name Dr. Romulus was a nod not only to Romulus, the founder of Rome, but also to invoke the idea of his twin brother Remus, with whom he suckled at the teat of a wolf as infants, and whom Romulus killed after their founding of Rome. I fully intended to use the word bifurcated later, and this split between founding patrician and fratricidal murderer was a subtle nod, a foreshadowing of language and of the murderous twist at the end of the song. Dr. Romulus also sounded like the name of a mad scientist super villain, which was exactly what I needed.

I drew inspiration from both *Dr. Horrible's Sing-Along Blog* and Jonathan Coulton's "Skullcrusher Mountain." I liked the accessibility and humanity of Dr. Horrible, but reveled in the unapologetic evil of Coulton's mad scientist, and tried to walk a line between the two, showing a slow progression. After all, he must be reasonable, right? He's calling the *Daily Journal* to complain, first, like any reasonable citizen. I considered having him write a letter to the editor, but the momentum and scansion of "Hello Daily Journal, connect me to Tom Evander, he wrote the piece today on Dr. Romulus" created an instant scene with characters and conflict utilizing a skillful efficiency of words. Someone is calling a newspaper, asking to be connected to a reporter, and both characters are introduced. Such efficiency in writing is incredibly valuable, so you can get to exploring the characters without getting dragged down in exposition.

The song gives a three-act play in just over 5 minutes. It tells an entire story, shows the arc, has a dynamic villain who grows ever more unhinged, all the while defending his horrible acts as a sort of moral pragmatism to achieve the same ends as the hero figure. Plus, there's the delicious wordplay, I get to hit some wonderful high notes, and let's not forget the robots.

I was caught off guard the first time someone in the audience voiced, "Yes!" after I sang, "Because of your transgressions you'll be torn apart by robots." In the recording, there is a hissed and slightly metallic, "Yes!" where I always envisioned the robots celebrating getting to do harm to someone with a choreographed fist pump. This was all head canon of my own devising, and I put it there entirely for me because it's what I heard in my head. Learning that people not only paid attention to my songs and recordings, but that they also truly enjoyed what seemed to me little in-jokes I placed just for myself was...heady.

It's not a perfect song, I know, and doubtless there are people who don't like it, but it's a song that a lot of people love, and one I'm ferociously proud of having written, not the least because of both the character development and wry, cerebral humor involved. Certain levels of humor take a higher level of effort, and planning, and though so much humor can be spontaneous, it is also subjective in the extreme. For every time a comedian throws out jokes with no seeming effort, especially really good jokes, there was more than likely a bit of preparation involved. Quality spontaneity requires more preparation than you'd imagine. Certainly, many funny jokes are made in the heat of the moment, but those are almost always dependent on the particular circumstance for context, and there will always be people in the room who thought it was forced or not funny, or worse, predictable.

Years ago, I got involved with a podcast called The Good Beer Show. On October 8, 2006, I was invited to sit in on a recording. I was a local musical comedian, and they were a podcast that reviewed beers and talked to local and regional musicians. I'd contacted them and we finally worked out a date for me to be on.

It was a good time. We drank beer from Oskar Blues, I made them laugh, and played three or four songs. The episode, (#93 "In The Can") aired the next day. The appearance was funny enough and our chemistry was right enough that I was asked back for a second appearance on May 27, 2007. And that one was a great time as well. I played more songs, and made more laughs, and on June 25, 2007, I began my stint as a regular on the Good Beer Show.

The Good Beer Show was an award-winning podcast that was the brainchild of Jeffrey T. Meyer, and it was during my stint on that show that I met Traci (who later became known as Cheeto-screech on the Beer Powered Time Machine podcast), Randy Davis, and Ty Morton. Traci and Randy were regular cast members of the Good Beer Show long before I joined. Ty started as a guest and also became a regular on the show.

When they asked my opinion, I gave it. The first time I had a sour beer (Moxie, from New Holland Brewing) I was asked what I tasted. Everyone else had used beer terms and tasted things I didn't. I was tempted to go along with the crowd and repeat some of the things I'd heard said, like a middle school student being asked to participate in a class discussion they didn't quite understand. Part of me railed against that, though.

Instead I said, "I dunno. It's tart, it's sweet, it's kind of vinegary but not, kind of fruity but not... Ketchup?"

Everyone laughed, and I felt like it was more at me than with me, but I laughed, too. That incident earned me the nickname (fair warning, it is on the offensive side) the Beer Tard, because I was unapologetic in my admission that I didn't know things.

Early on, I worked very hard in every episode to try and make people laugh, to do funny things. I prepared material or bits beforehand, waiting for a place in each episode to drop it in. Eventually I relaxed a bit, easing into the role of my offensive nickname. I asked questions when I had them, made jokes when I felt like it, and generally just acted like myself. Many times, I got thanked by other cast members for asking questions they felt too embarrassed to ask themselves.

But I'd stopped trying to make everyone laugh all the time. I remember once we had this local Indianapolis comic on the show, Otto. He's passed away, and he was a genuinely good person, but never made it far as a comic. Jeffrey T. loved him and talked up how he was the "hardest working comic in Indianapolis," who had done hundreds of shows in the past year, maybe even over 300. That was an impressive number, and I was too polite to point out that Otto hadn't got paid for the vast majority of them and had arranged most of the shows himself. Most of them were the equivalent of open mics, which, by the way, is fine and in no way undermines how much he was hustling, how much work he was doing. Maybe he was the hardest working comic in Indianapolis. He didn't have much to show for it, unfortunately, as hard work and commitment don't always equate into commercial success. I refuse to knock him in any way. I appreciated his comedy while understanding that it wasn't my preferred style and recognized his work ethic as being phenomenal.

But it was around this episode that Jeffrey T. started hinting that maybe he should get Otto on the show as a regular, that I wasn't cracking them up. At one point, he looked at me and said, "For a guy who makes his living as a standup comic, you are the least funny person I know."

I looked right back and said, "You aren't paying me to be funny. You aren't paying me at all."

It bothered me for a while, and then I let it go (well, to the extent that such a thing is possible for someone like me who obsesses over and is haunted by his shortcomings, missteps, and mistakes). When the Good Beer Show ended, it sort of ghosted into non-existence, which set the stage for me much later to start the Beer Powered Time Machine podcast with Ty and Randy and (occasionally) Trac—er—Cheeto-Screech, and all the others who joined us on the mics over the years, either as hosts or guests.

The time I spent with Jeffrey T. made me think about how I spoke to others. Sometimes I only think about it afterwards—and let's be fair: I fail a lot. I've failed a lot in life, at many things, including being a good person or a good example. In the past decade or so, I like to think I've made up a lot of that ground. I know I've tried. Maybe, like Otto, I don't have much to show for it, but I've put the work in.

I keep working on it, at least. In any case, I'll always be grateful to the Good Beer Show and Jeffrey T. for introducing me to the world and podcasting and expanding my understanding and appreciation of beer. I realize that any lessons I learned from that experience, or any experience, for that matter, were entirely my own to discern. I learned that the quickest, surest way to learn is to admit when you don't know something and ask. It spurred me to do the Beer Powered Time

Machine, to surround myself with people who like to make and do things, who will not only share in my joys, but share their joy as well. And I learned that you don't have to live up to someone else's expectations of you to find happiness or success.

Even if, for someone who made a living at standup comedy, I'm the least funny person Jeffrey T. has ever known.

(Not Quite) the Chosen One

Him and me, we're gonna save the day together. We will stand side by side forever.

Okay, I'm slightly behind him and out of the line of fire...

I know he is the face known everywhere, he gets the girls and the fanfare,

but when it comes down to the wire

He knows that he can't do it without me.

He doesn't have to say it and he probably never will...

But I keep his boots shined and cape well-pressed. I make sure he eats and gets his rest,

so he can shine like the sun.

And I keep his sword sharp and his horse well fed. I make his meals and I make his bed,

For I am the Chosen One...'s Assistant.

And when you pray to the gods, your lives to save from a dire and magic plague,

who do you think you're praying to?

Okay it's technically him, but who do you think gave him directions there, to a town out

in BFE nowhere,

Just so he could save save you?

'Cause I carry the maps and navigation equipment.

He looks good on a warhorse, but he can't even read...

But I, I hold the torch in dungeons deep, I tell him where he should storm the keep

so that the day gets won.

And I, I find the priest when there's undead, to bless his sword arm and helmet head,

For I am the Chosen One's Assistant.

I pitch the tents, I set up camp, I rub the knots from his toes when they cramp,

I stitch his wounds, I make repairs, mix winkle cream and pluck his thick nose hairs...

I pay off husbands when he sleeps with their wives, deflowered maidens when he ruins

their lives,

And who do you think cleans the dragon shit off the treasure?

It ain't him. No, he's out dancing at the balls, taking his bows and his curtain calls

while I'm in the stable

Alone with a book, and a lantern and stacks of scrolls, to learn how to beat three headed

trolls

Just so I'll be able

To tell him how to do it using small words and pictures.

And when he rescues that princess, do you think that he's gonna share?

But I, I swore an oath just to pay my rent, a strict non-disclosure agreement

So I can't tell anyone...

That he sleeps with a night light and sucks his thumb, he's bald as a rock and twice as

dumb,

For I am the Chosen One's Assistant.

(NOT QUITE) THE CHOSEN ONE

(N)ot Quite) The Chosen One" doesn't have much of an origin tale, no humorous, unbelievable, clickbait-worthy true story that inspired it. I just wanted to write a song about a person whose sole job is to make someone else look better in every way, act, word, deed, and appearance. I found the idea of telling the story of a grumbling assistant who signed a non-disclosure agreement in order to travel with a hero, and who has to not only do all the hero's menial tasks but also all of the research and prep work, and who also serves as a visual reminder of the hero's physical superiority, all while also covering up all of the hero's many physical, intellectual, and moral flaws, imperfections, and indiscretions interesting, and the writing of the song fell into place. I wrote it in an afternoon at the dining room table in late September or early October of 2013.

It's not a song that sprang from me whole cloth—I wasn't mugged by it, and the craft of songwriting played a fair hand in making it as well-written as it is, however well-written that may be, and I do happen to be pretty proud of having written it. I refer to it, in tone and general sound at least, as my Melissa Etheridge song. It's got that feel to it, the pulsing strums, the scansion, the low, half-spoken/half-sung verses that build and explode into soaring vocals on the choruses, the bridge that keeps moving and building into another climax which is accentuated by an immediate stop—a full measure of silence where all you can hear is the reverberation of the instruments, and then starts back again, building from the low pulsing strums through the chorus and into a melodic coda to resolve the song.

As far as songwriting or concepts go, it's not a particularly original song either in content or style. The subject has been tackled before, maybe better, and the song is pretty straightforward and mainstream 90's rock. The hardest part of writing the song, for me, was naming it. Most people refer to it as "The Chosen One's Assistant" or, on the occasion that they remember that that's not the title, "Not The Chosen One." I was struck by the comedic impulse to not give the joke away, not to telegraph the punch too much. I figured calling it "The Chosen One's Assistant" would be too obvious, too on the nose.

But then, I was the kid who grew up poring over album covers and through album inserts while listening to the albums, compulsively, looking for clues and secrets, obscurities and little idiosyncrasies, and I'm making music for a world who spent the 90s, the CD era, calling a song "Track 5" unless they'd heard the title on the radio a million times (or now, seen the title on social media a million times,) because it was track 5 on the CD. It's a little different now, with social media and streaming media seeming to return to an era of big singles being released as opposed to albums.

We live in a more obvious world now, a world where they feel the need to telegraph the punch to make you pay attention, because many people won't just listen to something to see if they enjoy it unless they already believe they're going to enjoy it, so you have to make sure they know they're going to enjoy it before they start, which means being overt and blunt with your titling and messaging. I'm a sort of musical Don Quixote operating with the chivalry of nuance in a world of bumper stickers and twitter messages and memes. There is less and less room for nuance every day, in many ways. But I'm rambling now...

It's been an inspiring song—not in a Bette Midler "Wind Beneath My Wings" way, not a song that makes people feel better or more confident, but in a creative way. It's a song that makes people want to create, to write about it, to use as the basis for something else creative. I've discussed it in panels on storytelling and character development at conventions. I've had people prepare and run "how to be a faithful sidekick" panels at conventions, based on the song. I've had several authors, aspiring and otherwise, ask to write it as a short story or novelization, including one, Kimber Grey, who is actually, actively doing just that (and who, coincidentally, isn't naming her book "(Not Quite) The Chosen One." Go figure).

It's been a more popular song than I figured it would, and has a broader appeal than I thought it would, and has plenty of spots for performance humor. I'm very fond of it in a way that doesn't always happen with a song—probably more than fond of it—I'm satisfied by it. It's one of those songs I can look at and think, "Ok. I put in good work." I hope to have more moments like that in my life, more songs like that in my life—hopefully many more.

When I think of "(Not Quite) The Chosen One," it's hard not to relate it to a career in standup comedy. In many ways, they're similar pursuits. In one, someone runs around trying to convince people they're a hero or a savior of sorts, and in the other someone runs around trying to convince people that they're funnier than anyone else. Both people spend inordinate periods of time traveling to get to the next gig, the next crisis, the next destination.

Sometimes the dates run together when you're working comedy. Sometimes the venues blur together. Sometimes the dates and venues and stories swap places in your head. Multiply this by more than a decade in the business, and it can be pretty tough, sometimes, to narrow down a specific date or venue for a story. And if the venue is a casino? It can be even worse, because casinos are, by and large, the same. In general, they're full of older people, lots of smoke, and emit a kind of desperate positivity, hell-bent on convincing you that you're not throwing your money away, risking your fixed income or retirement or paycheck or savings or house payment or whatever. I'm not opposed to the idea of casinos. I'm also not thrilled with the execution.

There are a few things that I was almost guaranteed of when I played a casino gig:

1. I'd get a buffet pass, and there'd be a mix of fantastic food, iffy food, and great tasting but horrible-for-me desserts,
2. I'd end up in a hotel room that smelled like smoke, whether or not it was designated as non-smoking
3. The pay would be pretty good, even though
4. I probably wasn't going to sell any merchandise because
5. I'd either be playing in a nightclub targeting specials to get local young people in, who were mostly trying to get drunk and pick someone up, or
6. I'd be playing in an auditorium full of older people taking a break from gambling, and most likely losing, and
7. I was going to be searched by security at least twice.

That last part isn't so bad for most comics, but it was always more of a hassle for me, being a guitar comic. To get into the casino, if you have a bag—any bag, purse, backpack, whatever—it has to be searched. I'd be going in with a guitar in a gig bag on backpack straps, a suitcase full of merchandise (because you never know, so you always pitch your merch), and a guitar stand. I had to answer questions from security at every casino I went in, had to let them look in every pocket of every bag on the way in, and then do it again when I was loading out of the casino. I know the guards didn't want to do it, either, but searching bags was their job, just like making people laugh was mine. I didn't resent them for it at all, but it was a hassle nonetheless. Still, the pay was pretty good, and I'd get a decent meal, or at least 12 decent desserts out of it, and it kept me in the good graces of bookers, and they kept dates on the books, so... I worked casinos.

In March of 2014, I was working at the Odawa Casino in Petoskey, MI. I played there two or three times in my career, and the venue was the Ozone Nightclub in the casino. I'm pretty sure this happened there, though I can't be sure, because it was at a casino and they, as I said before, are largely the same. I remember driving around, looking for something to eat and stopping at a Taco Bell for some reason, but did the story I'm about to tell happen there? It's a toss-up. It might have been Firekeeper's casino in Battle Creek, and I think it was, but my records indicate that I only worked there once, in 2011, although I'm certain I played there at least twice, and this incident seems more recent than that to me, but then is 2014 really that much more recent than 2011?

And does it matter? What matters was I played a show and had a sound guy—a dedicated sound technician for the room. Those are a luxury for a guitar comic, as we're more likely to ask who's running sound and be told that the head server knows how to turn on the PA if we know how to work it, but casinos tend to have sound people. Anyway, the sound guy, Tim (I can't forget that, even if I wanted to), asked if I wanted monitors.

Monitors are little speakers on the stage pointed at the musician so they can hear what they're doing. I said sure, why not? So we did soundcheck, and I sounded amazing. It was easily the best mix I'd ever heard of myself in my entire standup career. Tim knew what he was doing. We finished setup and I went and ate, then went back to my room to piddle around until closer to showtime. As always, I wanted to double check that the equipment was working before I went on, so I asked Tim for a quick check, and he turned the monitors on for me so I could do that. Everything was perfect. Showtime came and Tim announced me from the booth (there was no opener or feature that night, just a one-man show) and then I watched him leave the booth and go talk to a young woman for most of the rest of my show. It didn't matter to me. I was onstage and I sounded amazing.

Most of the room, however, didn't seem to be reacting to my act. I wrote it off to it being a casino gig, poured even more energy into my performance, and the folks up front, who were already into what I was doing, loved it even more. It was like this the entire evening, with me not feeling any energy from the audience except from the very front, the back of the room getting louder and louder, me pouring more and more energy into the performance. Then it was over and I came offstage. Tim still hadn't come back to the booth. A couple from the front row was enthusiastic as they bought a CD and a t-shirt, and told me it was the best comedy show they'd ever seen, anywhere. I got a beer after I tore down and asked the bartender if there was always this little response from the crowd. He said the audience couldn't hear me.

I was dumbstruck. I walked over to the sound booth and looked behind it, and Tim only had the monitors on for my inputs. The first couple of rows, the ones right next to the stage, could hear me just fine, and so could I, but Tim hadn't put my microphone and guitar back in the room speakers after that equipment check before the show, so most of the audience couldn't hear what I was doing, and I really didn't get to enjoy the fruits of what was undoubtedly the best sounding show of my comedy career.

Tim, man. Frickin' Tim. I've always been wary of stage monitors after that, even though I know in my heart it was the guy who walked away from his job that ruined that show for me. The Chosen One's assistant, if you catch my drift. I guess it's not just important to learn a lesson, but to understand which lesson you should learn. While I was wary of monitors because of this, what I was more aware of was communicating with the sound people when I had a sound crew to work with, making sure we're on the same page, always being friendly and professional, but also paying attention to whether or not the whole audience could hear me.

Still, though, I sounded amazing, at least to me and the front row...

Grandma's Got A Girlfriend

My grandpa's in the ground, my grandma put him down...
    She caught him messin' around with younger women, you know.
    She didn't even think twice, just got him in her sights.
    The funeral was nice. Too bad he had to go

Messin' round with those younger girls.
    But Grandma doesn't care; she's on top of the world.
    Grandma's got a girlfriend now.
    Grandma's got a girlfriend. My grandma's got a girlfriend.

My grandma's done with men, she won't look back again.
    She made a brand new friend; they get along just fine.
    Met at a rally in May, moved in the very next day.
    They watch the LPGA, they both like women and wine.

Heard Katy Perry singing "I Kissed A Girl,"
    Grandma thought about it, said she'd give it a whirl.
    Grandma's got a girlfriend now.
    Grandma's got a girlfriend. My grandma's got a girlfriend.

Gram says girls are where it's at,
    and now she's votin' Democrat.
    She dropped out of the NRA,
    Now she DJ's at a rave.
    Grandma's got a girlfriend. My grandma's got a girlfriend.

She's wearing tube socks with Birkenstocks,
    Got a brand new rainbow tattoo,
    And matching motor wheelchairs
    For her and her Boo,
    She had a handicapped ramp put on her closet just so she could
come out!

MIKEY MASON

Grandma's got a girlfriend, now.

GRANDMA'S GOT A GIRLFRIEND

G randma's Got a Girlfriend" was written in the months that led up to the *Dangerous Gifts* album in 2013, and I remember doing the writing in two different sessions— one up in my room—my secret lair— and the other at the dining room table. This was back in late April or early May, something I know because I did some of the first guitar tracking at the Loony Bin condo in Tulsa, OK, in late May of 2013.

This was one of those songs I wrote when I was considering material that might, somehow, cross over from my regular standup act to my geeky act and vice versa, back when I was still juggling two acts and the thought of merging them, as opposed to divorcing them and picking only one direction. Somewhere in the back of my head, I believed I could make a go of doing more intellectual, geeky comedy for a mainstream, middle-America audience. I still believe I could, but the truth is, I just didn't want to put in the volumes of work it would require. I'd rather put all that effort toward making music for the audience who already understood me.

Lyrically, this song was one of those doomed efforts to conjoin the two audiences. There's some lighthearted stereotyping involved on both sides of the fence here, mingled in some dark humor, and brought back around to a smirking sort of proselytizing. The song opens with Grandpa dying, and how? Grandma shot him for messing around with younger women. She got him in her sights, didn't even think twice, the funeral was nice, too bad he had to go messing round with them younger girls.

The joke seems to be that right-wing, NRA Grandma kills Grandpa, and then, after hearing "I Kissed A Girl," by Katy Perry, "turns" lesbian, rejecting all her former right-wing ways, "she dropped out of the NRA, now she DJs at a rave." There's at least one really good line in the song, and that's "she had a handicap ramp put on the closet just so she could come out."

Beyond that, I'm not surprised that it drew a lot of blank stares from middle America. My instincts were that those with right-wing predispositions would get a couple laughs out of the juxtaposition, but the reality was, the subtext (and it is barely subtext, it's pretty right on top of everything) of this song is "smash the patriarchy and do what is right for you." To do that in the song, Grandma used a lame justification for killing Grandpa—his infidelity. In certain states known for their right-wing attitudes—I'm looking at you Texas—it was legal as recently as 1973 for a man to kill his wife if she committed adultery. It still gets widely joked about. So my flipping the script, and putting the power (and the gun) in Grandma's hands in a boys-will-be-boys world, drew a lot of blank stares and polite applause.

People who love the song *love* it, but most either are made uncomfortable by it or don't give it too much thought. I don't think it wouldn't have worked on another album. *Dangerous Gifts*, with one single exception, is an album of dark humor, and this song was written as a sort of companion to "Mama's Goin' Dancing"—the country rock vibes and styles gel together nicely. Musically, this album, and specifically this song and "Mama's Going Dancing," were among my first attempts to play lead guitar on one of my comedy albums, although technically that honor goes to the title track of the *Storm Coming* EP, a decidedly not-comedy work recorded in early 2013 and released in April of 2013, just a month before I laid down the tracks to this song.

I'm proud of the lead guitar work I did on these songs. I just wish I'd continued practicing it, working at it, and developing it; but the reality is, my primary focus is on the songwriting. When it comes time for a solo, I'm either cobbling it together at the last minute or farming the work out to someone else, and let's face it, I have a great group of musicians willing to do that work for me. Still, this song, and a few others, remind me that I can do more if I want to, if I put my mind and fingers to it. That I can manage the solos without being a lead guitarist of any real sort gives me hope, in a way, that maybe it is possible for me to fuse together an act that would reach a median audience while maintaining the artistic, moral, and ethical integrity for the music I want to make, *if* I wanted to. As of this writing, that's still a level of effort I'm unwilling to make for an outcome I'm not sure I care enough to achieve, because I know what it would take. It's an inadvertent lesson I taught myself as a kid, one that I would repeat to my kids time and again.

I was fourteen or fifteen years old. We were poor and lived in a sprawling trailer park on the county line, pretty far from everything else. I had a bike when I was younger, a beat-up old bicycle, but it was out of commission by the time high school rolled around. This was sometime in 1988 or 89, and I decided for some unknown reason that I wanted to go to the mall and hang out. I have no idea why. I didn't have any friends there. I didn't have any money to spend. I just wanted to *do* something, and there was nothing for me right at that moment in the dilapidated, aging trailer park, so I decided to walk to the mall.

It was mid-afternoon when I started walking. I lived near the back of the trailer park, about a ten-minute walk from the entrance, and the mall was three and a half miles from the entrance of the trailer park. I know because I just looked it up before writing this sentence, because we live in the future and I can do that. Google says the walk takes about an hour, which might be factual if you got to walk straight there on a well-paved sidewalk with no interruptions. When you take into consideration that there are very few actual sidewalks along the way, and that you have to cross a couple of major intersections and a state highway, all of them divided by medians and all without cross-walks, it was closer to between an hour and a half and two hours.

With my trusty Walkman and a couple of cassette tapes, I kept my head down and walked to the mall with my long hair, blue jeans, and a jacket in the early summer mid-afternoon. I always wore a jacket. It was a thing. Both of my sons have gone through the same thing with hoodies, and as a parent it's a little frustrating, but on another level, I can't help but understand. It was hot. It was a long walk, much longer than I was used to, but I got to the mall.

I remember feeling a sense of accomplishment, of victory. I'd made it to the mall. But, like I said, I wasn't meeting anyone there, and I didn't have any money, so I went in, used the bathroom, got a drink from a water fountain, looked around the music store and the Spencer's gifts, then realized there wasn't much to do here but walk around and buy stuff. I couldn't buy stuff, and I didn't feel like walking around—I'd just walked three and a half miles. I sat down and rested for a few minutes in the air conditioning, then turned around, put my headphones back on and started walking home. I didn't even have a quarter to call home for a ride, not that it would've done me any good. Mom was at work. There wasn't a ride to be had.

So I started walking back. It was late afternoon now, and the sun gave everything an orange-gold tint as I walked. My sweat held the hair closest to my skin to the back of my neck as I walked, and I still remember the songs I listened to on repeat: listen, rewind, listen, because they had good walking beats. To this day, I still can't hear "Partners in Crime" or "I'm a Legend Tonight" off of KISS' *Killers* without thinking about walking down County Line Road.

There were times I wanted to stop, where I wished I had a ride and thought about trying to hitchhike, but I knew in the back of my head the only way I was getting home was to keep putting one foot in front of the other, and I told myself I should just be glad it was cooling off as the sun was going down. It was full dark by the time I made it back to the trailer park, and I was pretty tired. The batteries on my Walkman were dead before I got all the way home.

I sat there for a while, alone, thinking about what I'd done. I felt empowered. I was able to pick a place and get there, to pick a task and accomplish it on my own. On the other hand, the task, the accomplishment, they felt meaningless in and of themselves. Sure, I walked to the mall. But what did I really get out of it? I never walked to the mall again.

In retrospect, what I got out of it was the knowledge that I could do things; that I had choices, that I could take action, create a plan and follow through. What I got out of it was the knowledge that the path to any destination was made of single steps that even a kid could take. Sure, there are millions of ways to get where you're going, but you can get there by walking if you were determined enough, and that was all I had available to me, then.

No, I never walked to the mall again, but I walked other places. To other neighborhoods to visit friends. To closer stores, when I had a little pocket money. I'd figured out that if I was going to put the work in, I should have a more defined goal and reason, a purpose for the work. That philosophy held true much later when I decided to be a standup comic. I kept my head down and moved steadily towards that goal. I didn't get distracted, didn't turn around, didn't stop for a breather. I just kept working toward it. That philosophy is what I've tried to teach my sons, every time I tell that story to them, and especially when they have long homework assignments that seem impossible to finish. I tell them they are not impossible, just long, and they can only get to the end of them by taking each step through them.

I could have learned a different lesson from that experience. I could have learned no lesson at all. Lots of people don't. I don't know if that's because of luck, or genetics, or learned behaviors, or what. But I am glad it wormed its way into my head, grateful that I can see a series of steps instead of vast distances or far-flung destinations, that I can break bigger goals down into smaller pieces that I can do and not remain overwhelmed by mere the thought of the larger goal.

It's why I have this career.

Waste 'Em With My Crossbow

Same old song, night after night and there's nothing near it.
    Wait so long, the music the dice make, I love to hear it.

Whether it's a dwarf with a sucking chest wound,
    Or Return to the Temple of Horrendous Doom,
    Or a swack iron dragon, we just bust in the room and
    Hoody Frickin' Hoo!

Fireball's coming online, B.A.
    Sara just sighs cause we won't parley,
    I grab my trusty Hackmaster +12 and hear Bob say...
    "I waste 'em with my crossbow!"

Time moves slow. I drag through the work week to get to tonight and
    Here we go. My sheet's on the table, I'm ready to fight and,

Whether we're running from the Doomsday Pack,
    Or in Muncie's steam tunnels, braving the black,
    Or another Bag War 'cause Barringer's back, it's...
    Hoody Frickin' Hoo!

13

WASTE 'EM WITH MY CROSSBOW

Back when my ex-wife and I first split, when my oldest was around three years old, they moved three hours away to be with her family. It wasn't always easy, getting back and forth. Back then, I wasn't a stand-up comic yet, and three hours seemed like a long drive. Now my butt doesn't even start to fall asleep until around the five-hour mark, but anyway… When Jody and I got together, she would often undertake this drive with me—it was incumbent upon us to make the full three-hour drive both ways, most times. Occasionally, we'd get met about two hours away. I won't get into it. It's the past.

In the meantime, I had discovered a comic series called *Knights of the Dinner Table* by Jolly Blackburn. It was set in Muncie, IN, the city in which I lived then, and do again now, and was about tabletop role-playing gamers around the general area of my alma mater, Ball State University. The main characters (BA, Bob, Dave, Sarah, and Brian) spoke to me, and at times *for* me, and reflected a genuine love and life-time of experience playing role-playing games.

While Jody wasn't a gamer, she'd grown up hanging out with gamers, witnessing the games, hearing their gaming stories and arguments and all the minutiae and periphery that comes with being the kind of adolescents who sit around a table drinking soda, reading books, rolling dice, getting somewhat overly emotionally invested in said dice rolls, and doing math on a Saturday night for fun (and yes, that is a rudimentary, bare-bones description of role-playing games. It leaves out a lot, like the group storytelling and the laughing and the fun, the Monty Python references and so, so much more, but back to the story...).

I'd buy these comic books, very word-dense comic books with simple art and story lines centered around a gaming table, and I'd read them to Jody while she drove the two to three hours or so to pick up Ben. I had voices for each character, so I never had to tell her who was talking, at least not when it was just the primary group of 5 characters. We'd laugh and discuss the comics and offer up stories and memories of our own, and it made this boring drive waiting to see my son bearable. It's fair to say that I brought some emotional baggage to my personal investment in those books and those characters, but that doesn't change the fact that I loved them.

Flash forward more than a decade to late February of 2014. I'd been a stand-up comic for a decade or so, was in the transition to becoming a professional geek entertainer, and set to make an appearance at VisionCon. I'd been attending VisionCon for a couple years in Springfield, MO, but by 2014 it had moved to Branson. I was a Guest of Honor, along with Ernie Hudson—yes, that Ernie Hudson. He was gracious and I did an interview with him and I geeked out over him. I'd talk about him more, but this story isn't about him. Another Guest of Honor was Jolly Blackburn, the creator, writer, and artist of the *Knights of the Dinner Table*. To say that I was looking forward to that weekend would be an understatement.

Less than a week before the convention, I learned that there was going to be a live-action KODT web series, and I was super-excited. There was a Kickstarter for it and Jolly was involved, and I knew in my heart that if it was going to happen, *I* wanted to write the theme song. So, I did what I normally do: I dove into it head-first and started writing. I wrote and recorded the demo of "Waste 'Em With My Crossbow," and on February 26th, 2014, posted it as an unlisted video on YouTube and a sent a blind DM to Jolly on Facebook, explaining who I was, that I'd be at VisionCon with him as a fellow Guest of Honor, and asking him to listen to the song.

He responded that he was on the road, but had listened and thought it was awesome, that we'd talk later, and he thanked me. That weekend, while I was on the road driving to VisionCon, I ended up on a Skype call with Jolly and Ken—the director of the live-action series. Spoilers—it was ill-fated. But... they loved my song, wanted to use it as the theme song, and wanted me to write another, AC/DC-style song for the series. That ended up being "Roll The Dice," and also appeared on the *dodecahedron* album.

My booth at the convention was just a couple over from Jolly's, and his wife Barb and I talked off and on throughout the convention. It was a fantastic weekend. He appreciated how the song showed a true and thorough understanding of the characters in the comic, situations in which those characters had been placed, and running jokes. And I told him about my history with the comic (well—an abbreviated history).

Although the live-action series never got the production it deserved (the actors were incredible, the director/producer not so much), Jolly and I have stayed in touch. Last year, we were both Guests of Honor at InConJunction in Indianapolis, and I got to participate in a live reading of the comic in front of Jolly as part of a panel. When I told the story on the panel, they wanted to hear the voices. I'll never forget the look on Jolly's face when he heard me doing each one. It was priceless.

As for the song itself, the writing was pretty straightforward, with a driving, fanboyish energy. That's me playing lead guitar, which is something I've done on only a fraction of the tunes in my catalog. Since I'm not terribly good at playing lead guitar, I tend to record it in little bits and edit them together to create a cohesive solo. There might be 10 different takes edited together there. At DragonCon, someone asked if I'd purposefully included the nod to the theme song from the 1980s *Buck Rogers* TV show in the solo. I didn't know what they were talking about, but had loved the show as a kid. I hopped online and listened to the theme song, and there it was. Super-similar rising riff present in both. So maybe that was subconscious (but in reality, I was just playing with intervals and pacing in the solo, and thought it sounded cool.) Any way it goes, every time I hear the song, I sit there smiling, thinking, "That was me. I did that." I'm very proud of that solo.

Someday, I'll get to perform this song live in front of a whole room of KODT fans, but to date that hasn't happened yet. There are almost always one or two fans of the books in every audience of mine, but I long for the day when I'll be singing the solo and be met with a thunderous, "Hoody Frickin' Hoo!" It would bring the story full circle.

"Waste 'Em With My Crossbow" is only one example of the way our daily lives inform and influence our artistic and professional lives. In fact, I might even owe my entire career in standup comedy to one such instance. And luckily enough, sometimes things do get to come full circle in this huge, tiny world.

Back before I was ever on the road as a stand-up comic, or a professional entertainer of any sort, I was, like many people, a college student. In December of 1994, my sister Tina and brother-in-law Chad took me and my on again/off again high school girlfriend to a comedy club in Greenwood, Indiana. We saw an act there that we'd never heard of. I had forgotten their name for a long time, though I remembered it much, much later. It was a guitar act, a musical comedy duo. I had just turned twenty-one and we had a wonderful time that night, and I remember watching them the entire night, despite the fact that I was having a great time, thinking, "I could do that. I could do that."

"I could do that. I could do *that* for a living."

There was one specific bit they did that stuck with me for some reason, though for a long time, more than a decade, even, I didn't remember that it was them who did it. They had a bit where they sang a parody of the song "Bingo" just for a verse.

"There was a man who had no tongue and Ahh-yahh was his name-o. Ahh-yahh, yah-yah-yah. Ahh-yahh, yah-yah-yah. Ahh-yahh, yah-yah-yah, and Ahh-yahh was

his name-o!"

For whatever reason that cracked me up at 21 years old, and for years afterwards, I'd repeat it to make people laugh. I couldn't recall where I heard it. I just assumed it was Robin Williams because it sounds like the kind of thing Robin Williams would have done. I went back to school and within a year or two I had started writing notes, ideas for a stand-up act. It was bad, and that's being generous. But I decided I could do that for a living, you know, like you do. I just didn't act on it, not for years, at least.

More than a decade later, 2008 comes around and I'm working the Comedy Zone at the Atlantis Resort and Casino in the Bahamas for two weeks. I met the other comic, DC Malone, just before the first show of the run. He was another guitar act, which is weird because bookers don't tend to want to put guitar acts together, they prefer to work specialty acts (musical acts, ventriloquists, magicians, or prop acts) with monologists—comedians who just talk into a microphone and nothing else. As a general rule, they don't work two specialty acts together, especially not two acts of the same type, but there'd been a cancellation. DC was available, and they just rolled with it. When showtime arrived, I went up and did my act—I was featuring. After I came offstage, I spent the rest of the show back in the booth watching him do his act and there was just something familiar about this guy, something I couldn't place until, out of nowhere, he bursts into a quick, energetic song parody.

"There was a man who had no tongue and Ahh-yahh was his name-o. Ahh-yahh,

yah-yah-yah. Ahh-yahh, yah-yah-yah. Ahh-yahh, yah-yah-yah, and Ahh-yahh was

his name-o!"

I just lost it in the back, memories from years ago flooding to the forefront of my mind. It was him. DC Malone was part of the duo that I had seen onstage my first time at a comedy club. I was working a comedy show with one of the guys whose live act convinced me in my head that I could do this for a living, and here I was doing it for a living.

I didn't say anything to him that night, I just sold merch, exchanged pleasantries, and went back to my room. I talked with Jody by text—we weren't calling as often as usual because it was an expensive international call. I told her about it, and she was getting excited for me because this was kind of like meeting my comedy dad in a way. Not really, but if we were a sitcom, that would have been my comedy dad. I looked him up online and found out the duo's name had been Malone and Nootcheez. It took me a couple days, but eventually I brought it up with him. I didn't want to seem creepy.

I was tentative, saying, "Okay, so this is gonna sound weird, but..." and then I started the story from the beginning. It came burbling out in a garbled mess of memories and awkward emotions, and he laughed. We ended up becoming pretty good friends on that trip. We talked about it a lot, joked about him being my comedy dad a lot. We sat on his balcony and drank bottle after bottle of Jameson Whiskey, because he had a much better view than I did. We explored the islands, hung out, we had adventures together.

It was a great time, fantastic and strange. It turned out that the other half of that group, Nootcheez, had retired maybe a decade earlier, and was doing mundane work somewhere because he didn't want the road life anymore. I think he got married and had a day job, and was very happy. They were still in touch. DC now lives in the Pacific Northwest and we still talk occasionally, though we're not close. The whole experience was just this wonderful, remarkable coincidence showing me how big and how small the world is all at once.

Mythologist Joseph Campbell once wrote, "Follow your bliss. If you do follow your bliss, you put yourself on a kind of track that has been there all the while waiting for you, and the life you ought to be living is the one you are living. When you can see that, you begin to meet people who are in the field of your bliss, and they open the doors to you. I say, follow your bliss and don't be afraid, and doors will open where you didn't know they were going to be. If you follow your bliss, doors will open for you that wouldn't have opened for anyone else."

Working with DC in the Bahamas just felt like the universe telling me, "Yeah, this is what you're supposed to do. You took the hint, thank you, and now you've come full circle. Welcome to where you're supposed to be, or at least to the path that you're supposed to be on."

It makes me feel that this is a beautiful, weird world built of concentric circles and Venn diagrams, and loops and turns, and no-one can see it all.

Maybe life is like a Magic Eye™ picture from the 1990s. You have to kind of look past it and through or beside it, or get closer and move farther away slowly, try to catch it at just the right angle. Then, sometimes, you get a glimpse of the picture. I don't know. I don't necessarily believe in destiny, but it did feel like I was looking at this Magic Eye™ picture and just for a moment, everything snapped into perfect clarity and focus and I could see the boat or the horse or whatever it is in that auto stereogram.

The world can be magical place. It is a huge world, a tiny world. It is full of dichotomies and beauty and pain and hilarity and tragedy. Reach out and grab it and find where you're supposed to be. Keep looking at that picture and someday I hope it snaps into focus just like it did for me. And then look again, somewhere else, with a different perspective. Always keep looking.

LYRICS - THE CURSE

The Curse

It doesn't matter where you are, when there's a man with a guitar
    Somebody watching, be they hick or jock or nerd,
    Wants to be funny but they just can't find the words.
    It's like a plague that we all face... A dire curse cast upon the
human race.
    At every open mic, recital or concert,
    There's some jackass who shouts, "Freebird!"

And it's not limited to us, Those few guitarists who have not quit in
disgust,
    Great comic minds from Patton Oswalt to CK,
    Carlin and Hicks heard some
    douche say, "Freebird!"

Tell me just what it is that makes you think that line's so friggin' great?
    Tell me just what you need, what unexplored desire that you must
sate?
    Is it for attention or Asperger's or a lesion in your brain?

Where did Skynyrd touch you, how can we stop the pain?
Maybe with some Stairway? No?
Only one thing's gonna soothe your soul? Let's go!

On a mountain long ago shrouded in the mists of time,
 A man stood preaching, teaching others how to love and to be kind,
 And how the meek they shall inherit all the earth,
 Then Judas stood and screamed, "FREEBIRD!"

When Nero fiddled... "Play Freebird!"
 Et tu brute? "Liberum Avis!"
 "Hey, Galileo! Play Free bird!"
 Give me liberty or give me—"Freebird!"
 Four score and seven—"Play Freebird!"
 The only thing we have to fear is "Freebird!"
 Blood, toil, tears and sweat—"FREEBIRD!"
 I have a dream... "Play Freebird!"
 Ask not what your country can-- "Shut up and play Freebird or we'll kill you!
 Mr. Gorbachev, tear down that—"Freebird!"

14

THE CURSE

T he Curse" is one of those songs I almost wish I hadn't written. It's frustrating, because I love it and it's a good song. In fact, it's probably (from an artistic, musical, and writing standpoint, and this is just my opinion, so take that for what it's worth), the best song about "Freebird" that has been written, that may ever BE written.

And that's the problem. People know that I, as an artist, hate when people at a show yell "Freebird" from the audience. Some audience members think it's an act, but I'm here to tell you that regardless of who you are, no artist (and most audience members) *wants* you to shout "Freebird" at a performance. None. Certainly not me. I can't think of any. Zero. Including Lynyrd Skynyrd. None. Not even comedians who have a bit or a song about it.

The simple truth is this: if you shout "Freebird" at a show, I genuinely like you less than I did before the show. That's the most brutally honest, yet diplomatic way I can state it. If you care about a performer's feelings, the flow of their show, their set list, the hours, weeks, and years they spent writing and rehearsing, if you respect them AT ALL, you'll keep this tired, hackneyed bit of dead, overly-beaten horse dung out of your mouth.

I want you to understand that I am neither kidding nor overreacting. My words are measured and planned, my tone even-keeled. I'm not ranting or name-calling. This is neither hyperbole nor exaggeration. I don't want you to do it. Ever. No artist does, ever, and if you do, you are communicating to them and everyone around you that you care more about you and that horrid, weakass joke than you do anyone else or the show. True story. Tell your friends. Please.

Anyway, the most frustrating part about having written a song that is clever, and musically interesting, but that does not say "Freebird" in the title is that whenever someone brings up songs about "Freebird," they never bring up yours. Invariably, they will bring up the Doubleclicks' "The Guy Who Yelled Freebird," which, while an amusing enough song, and having "Freebird" right there in the title, lacks the same punch, either from a musical or writing standpoint, that "The Curse" has. Full disclosure: that is entirely my opinion, and I do not require or expect anyone else to share it. It is not meant to imply that the Doubleclicks aren't awesome. They unequivocally are awesome, and they probably know more about writing, marketing, and titling songs in today's musical environs than I do.

It makes me rethink trying harder, trying to be subtle, trying to expand my musical vocabulary, trying to do something different. It makes me think I should name every song exactly what it is, because otherwise people won't pay attention. And, as an artist, I don't like that, and I never have. I originally wanted to name my song "Great Pumpkin" from the *Driven* album "Okay, Maybe." I still think that's a stronger title, but I also know that even fewer people would have listened to it if I hadn't named it "Great Pumpkin."

But these things all fall solidly into the category of "my problem." I'm the creator. I cannot make people take notice, and when they do, I cannot force people to see my creations the same way I do, or to recognize the merits I see in them.

What I will say is that "The Curse," while seeming straightforward in its condemnation of people who yell "Freebird," proves to be lyrically complex and thematic, and builds upon that theme throughout the song in a way that many songs just don't. It also builds, has dynamic swells, and pulls from the original song that it lambasts in a thematically appropriate way, which also furthers the song. On top of that, the bass line at the beginning might be the best bass-work I've ever personally done on a song, and I did all the guitar work myself.

In any case, it's up to you to enjoy it, or not, to appreciate it, or not, in whatever way you will, or won't. My insecurities and idiosyncrasies are not your problem, and that is as it should be. I would play this song far more often live, except that it invariably increases the number of people who shout "Freebird," and who ask if I've heard someone else's song about "Freebird."

Which isn't (usually) what an artist wants. But being an artist isn't always about getting what you want, and always being successful at something doesn't necessarily make you the best artist you can be. If you're always doing well at everything you attempt, that's a sort of charm, but when you inevitably fail (and fail hard), then you'll also see it as sort of a curse, as well.

In February of 2015, I was doing my first stint at the MGM Northfield Hard Rocksino, working with Mike Armstrong, the cop-turned-comic who got famous on the Bob & Tom Show. The buffets were nice enough, and the shows were good, but the highlights of that week were seeing Paul Stanley's signed Ibanez guitar that he played in Cleveland on May 6, 2000, hanging on the wall of the casino, and then finding a dress of Tina Turners and a hat from Ike Turner, and realizing that they were about as far away from each other as two pieces of memorabilia could get in the casino. Like, on opposite sides of the casino. I found that funny.

But the most lasting impression of that trip was finding Stan's Northfield Bakery, a Polish and Czech bakery that was selling Paczki and introduced me to Kolacky (pronounced Koh-Lah-chee). I remember Cheap Trick on the radio as I drove out of there, fruit-filled pastry in hand, singing, "Your mama's alright, your daddy's alright. They just seem a little weird..."

I was headlining for the Comedy Zone, and they booked the Hard Rocksino gig, but they booked me there as a feature. I didn't care—it was decent pay. I was hoping the next time I'd be booked as a headliner, but it didn't work out that way. I'd been told to make an impression on the room manager, develop a relationship. This is something we try to do as comics, but also sometimes an exercise in futility, because for every manager of a room that stayed there, developing the business and carefully curating the performer rotation, there were five or ten who were replaced the next time you worked the room. Still, you do what you can.

I played the Hard Rocksino for the last time on the weekend of Friday and Saturday, January 29 and 30, 2016. I was featuring for Shaun Jones—a hilarious comedian who by all rights should be famous by now, but somehow isn't. I remember posting pictures from the green room. I'd just got Betsy, the guitar I still use, a Fender Hellcat, on my way to MarsCon in Williamsburg, VA, a week or so earlier and had set her up and sound checked her as usual, and was ready.

But when I was introduced... she didn't work. The battery was dead. It was an awkward moment, as I would always take the stage with bluster and bravado, grabbing my guitar right off the bat, asking the crowd if they were ready to rock. It was a casino crowd, who are fairly hard to predict as far as audiences go, but this one was a packed room and seemed ready and responsive and then... nothing. I put the guitar down—they couldn't hear it, so it wasn't worth it, and did my set. I had a lot of standup material at that point that wasn't songs and I only had to fill 20 minutes, but they just wouldn't bite. That first impression, the silent guitar, cost me the show. I lost the audience in the first minute and couldn't get them to buy in for the rest of my act. I bombed. Hard.

It was the hardest I'd ever bombed. I'd had bad shows before. Without bragging, there weren't a ton of them. I'd been doing comedy for eleven years at that point, and on the road as a full-time comic for about seven of them, and while I'd had bad shows, I never—never—had a show where I just couldn't make the audience laugh. The manager gave me the light, the sign to get offstage early. That's how silent it was. It was crushing, humiliating, and it was, I choose to believe, because the battery in my guitar died, and they didn't get to hear what my actual act was. It stays with you, that deafening kind of silence. It works into your soul.

It's one of those things I should have experienced far earlier in my career. Most comics do. That's what the years of open mics are for, and the next years of emceeing. But I started as a feature act, a middle act. I skipped steps, years, maybe a decade because I just happened to have the chops and the material. I thought that I'd been good enough, or lucky enough, or some combination of both, to never have to deal with it, but I've realized since that the lucky ones are most likely the ones who experience the failures early on and figure out how to persevere, and cope and work through it. When you're 11 years in and you bomb—truly bomb—for the first time, you are simply not emotionally prepared for the experience. I know I wasn't.

It was devastating, one of the hardest moments of my professional comedy career. The rest of the shows that weekend were fine, even great. I left the venue and bought new batteries during Shaun's set that first night and had a fresh battery every show for the rest of the weekend. My guitar worked. But the audiences were light, and even though I was received well, I was certain the manager's mind would always reflect back on those painful, silent 20 minutes in his packed room.

When September came, I was supposed to start booking comedy gigs for the next year, but didn't, although it wasn't because of the Rocksino experience—it turned out I already had a full calendar of conventions and online shows. I had five full-length geeky albums, an EP, and several singles. I'd begun the transition from full-time standup comic to full-time geek entertainer in earnest. That audience taught me a lesson, though, and one I should have learned and come to terms with long before, and thought I had (though now I know I hadn't).

It's important to fail so you have the coping mechanisms associated with it. It's important to fail so your perseverance means something. If you begin an endeavor as a success and just keep succeeding, never failing, never facing a setback that makes you question your worth, your desire, whether it's worth it to keep doing this thing you're doing? That doesn't take anywhere near the guts, the determination of someone who knows what those failures feel like but keeps coming back.

I'm not saying that you should sabotage yourself, but failing for the first time early in your career isn't nearly the same as failing for the first time once you've established your career and built something. Part of me is glad I didn't fail early on—I genuinely question if I'd have had the endurance, the determination to keep going, to continue in the face of failure. Part of me wishes that I knew how that would've played out. It's a moot point, now, anyway, but still worth considering.

I'm not sure I want to know the answer, though.

Last Day At Work

This was my last day at work. I'm moving on to a new employer,
  And better pay and better perks. This was my last day at work.

So I showed up in old pajamas,
  which was actually pretty thoughtful considering that I sleep in the
nude.
  I filled my car's trunk with office supplies, and posted drunken
  naked Office Christmas Party antics on YouTube.
  This was my last day at work.

I took a nap underneath my desk.
  My boss was late and so I urinated in every one of his potted
plants
  Then I loosened all the screws on his chair, gave his private bathroom an upper decker
  and shook everybody that I hated's hands (without washing mine.)

This was my last day at work... I'm moving on to a new employer,
  And better pay and better perks. This was my last day at work.
  I'm getting my own office with a window and best of all none of
these jerks .
  This was my last day at work.

And when I gave my farewell speech as I was standing on my desk,
screaming I am
  Spartacus, I actually convinced the new guy to quit his job and just
walk out.
  And then my phone rang in my pocket just as I was really raving.
  My new firm had just gone bankrupt, the doors were closing.I t
turned out
  This was my last day at work.

It was too late to apologize for changing my boss's out of office
reply to
   "I'll get back to you after I'm done with this young gigolo named
Miles."
   Or for setting his secretary's computer to autocorrect his name
To "Mr. Assless Chaps" and then deleting all her files.
   Or for locking the supply cabinet and shoving all the keys under-
neath the door.
   Not even the janitor will write a reference letter anymore (must've
been the upper
      decker.)

It was my last day at work. And that's how I began in comedy,
   Just one of life's little quirks. This was my last day at work.

LAST DAY AT WORK

L ast Day At Work" is a song that folks can relate to. Most of us have at least had little revenge fantasies about leaving the workplace in a dramatic scene, without hurting anyone, but at least getting that last upper hand, that final word and laugh in, and it's a song that somehow follows me. It is also the one successful song to cross over from my standup career into my geeky career, but it entered my life almost by accident.

My actual last day at work, the last day I worked for someone else at a "day job," was June 18, 2009. I'd worked at a residential placement facility for at-risk youth for just over a decade at that point, and though I don't think I'd ever go back there even if I somehow went back to working a straight job, it was a big enough part of my life that I actually dream about being back there, working again, on a semi-regular basis. I generally have one of those dreams every other month or so, sometimes more often.

In my dreams it's completely different and exactly the same, the way places are in dreams, and it's always a combination of over-whelming stress and feeling like home. It was a very supportive place that made all sorts of accommodations so I could follow my dreams and pursue performing as a career. It was incredible. They worked with me on paid and unpaid time off, let me drop from lower middle-management to another position as a part-time employee, and worked with my schedule even then. And when I planned a show and CD recording for the night of my last official day at work, my work family showed up in force, late in the evening. On a Thursday.

My third comedy album, *He Thinks He's Funny*, was recorded that night. I came up to the stage at Doc's Music Hall—it's closed, now, on its way to becoming a dance studio or a real estate office or something —to the sounds of Slayer's "Raining Blood." It was a great show, tremendous energy and everyone in high spirits, and when they asked for an encore, I did "Saturday Morning Cartoons," because I knew that was what they wanted. And when I finished that, they called for another encore, so I did "I Want To See Bea Arthur Nude."

Still, they wanted more, and I asked, "How do you follow that...?" What I actually said was, "What the hell else could you possibly want from me...?" I was tapped. There was nothing else to perform, nothing I wanted to perform or that I felt was worth performing, anyway. But the chanting didn't stop, so I made up a song.

That song was "Last Day at Work." It was not, by any stretch, what the final song ended up being. Years later, on May 6, 2014, I finalized and recorded what I thought would be a simple acoustic version at our kitchen table and released it on the FuMP (the Funny Music Project.) I added a reference to one of my favorite movies, *That Thing You Do!* with the "I am Spartacus" line. I figured I'd go back and re-record it, even re-write parts of it again, but on May 10, 2014 it got airplay on Dr. Demento's internet radio show/podcast, becoming the sixth song of mine the Doctor played, and has appeared on the Dr. Demento show eight times over the years, the most played song of mine by him. It was even nominated for a Logan Award.

I thought it was a throwaway. I couldn't have been more wrong. I ended up putting it on my *Red Letters* album, which was ostensibly an album about special days, 'red letter' days, but turned out to be an album about frustration, loss, cruelty, isolation, self-destructive behavior, and regret. It fit right in with both themes. It's one of those songs that still catches me off guard when people talk about it or ask me to play it, but I'm grateful, not only for that job and the support they showed me as a worker, but again as I made the transition to comedian, and the transition from there to finding my tribe and doing geeky music. I'm grateful this is my job now, and that people like the songs they like, even if I'm surprised by it—especially if I'm surprised by it. And I don't think I ever want to see my last day at work from this job.

That doesn't mean I didn't love my time as a comedian. It was an adventure and very educational, though maybe it foreshadowed what my career would become. In January of 2010, I performed for the second of three times in my life at the Loony Bin in Oklahoma City, OK. It was a week-long gig. There was a Wednesday show, a Thursday show, and two shows each on Friday and Saturday.

I remember the Loony Bin gigs for having nice comedy condos (in actuality they were well-maintained houses that the club owned and club staff would come in and clean after a comic left), and for being lenient about when you arrived or left the condo. They knew you lived on the road, and you could work all three Loony Bin rooms and never have to get a hotel out of your own pocket, spending three straight weeks on the road at their houses. They also had little notebooks in them that the comedians would sign or write messages about their week in, and some of them were quite old and from pretty famous people.

I remember that week because of who I was working with. I was the feature act—the middle—and he was the headliner. I won't name names, but I remember him very well. He was a comedian who performed mainly on cruise ships (and he talked about it a LOT, often in a belligerent manner, because he was drunk and angry most of that week). His performance style was a mixture of standup comedy and a little bit of a cappella singing and soft-shoe dance. Maybe he was only singing because I was a musical comedian. I don't know.

What I do know in my heart, though, was he hated following me. I was having a good week of performances, connecting well with the crowds and selling lots of merch after the shows. I was sure that this would be the week that got me bumped to headliner in that club—I was already headlining the other Loony Bins. When I say he hated me, I only say it because he spent a lot of time trying to tear me down at the condo—making fun of what I was wearing, making fun of my appearance, my act. And he was drunk. It was very much like dealing with an alcoholic, abusive parent. I kept my door shut and stayed in my room whenever I was in the condo.

He spent a lot of time at the club talking with the two owners who ran that club, he said they were friends of his, and I have a suspicion he's the reason I never headlined the room. I'm certain he badmouthed me to the club owners, even though I didn't even say anything when he straight up did a Bill Cosby bit onstage at the club —he did the Sick and Tired bit. I remember it from Cosby's "Himself" special. Where he's talking about his mother saying she was sick and tired. Cosby (and this guy ripping him off) said,

"And tired" always followed sick. Worst beating I ever got in my life, my mother said, "I am just sick..." And I said, "and tired." I don't remember anything after that.

Me? I didn't say anything. I just wanted to keep the peace, keep my head down, do a good job, and headline the next time I came back. But often it's not enough to do that in the comedy business. I won't complain about fairness—every business has its BS to deal with and I've had plenty of advantages, not the least of which was being a white male.

But he came back drunk again that night and tore into me. He was drunk and screaming that I didn't want to be a comedian, that I wanted to be a singer. He was very drunk and getting angrier by the minute. He repeated himself a lot, this guy who billed himself as Entertainer— literally had "Entertainer" in front of his name on his headshots, this guy who avoided the label comedian himself, screaming at me that I didn't want to be a comedian. That I was lying to myself. I thought he might hit me. I went to my room, shut and locked my door, and left early in the morning.

I only worked that room one more time, as part of a "triple feature" show—three feature acts, each doing twenty-five to thirty minutes with no closing act, no headliner. Maybe I never got to headline that room because he badmouthed me. Maybe I never headlined the room because they knew how he was, despite being friends with him, and I never called him out for plagiarizing Cosby's act, never complained about his abusive behavior. Maybe that was it, some sort of bizarre test. I don't know. But maybe, and this is the worst part, maybe somewhere down deep he was right. Maybe I really didn't want to be a comedian. Maybe I just wanted to be a singer. Anyone who pays attention to my act knows that I still do funny music, and also that I've been making the slow, steady shift towards more serious music as well. Maybe…

Maybe I owe him a thank you, for making me want to find something better, to be something more. Maybe, in some way, his drunken criticism, his constant harangue pushed me to be better than I was, truer to myself than I was. Maybe that weekend a year before "She Don't Like Firefly" was written, this "Entertainer" pushed me, unknowingly, towards embracing my geek side.

Maybe I owe him a drink. I don't know. I'll think about it. Until then, he'll have to remain in the category of That One Person. What's that? You don't know about That One Person? You should. You've been affected by them. We all have. It's unavoidable. We deal with the fallout of That One Person all the time. All. The. Time.

Look at any warning label, and you'll likely see the fallout of just one person: the label on the chainsaw that says "Do Not Hold Wrong End of Chainsaw," or on a jet ski that says "never use a lit match or open flame to check fuel level," the hair dryer that is labeled "do not use while sleeping," or those reflective cardboard sun shades for car dashboards that are labeled "do not drive with sun shield in place," or the irons with labels that read "do not iron clothes on body." You can almost guarantee that these have roots in at least one person (and hopefully just one person) doing something stupid, something that it should be obvious they shouldn't do, and then a lawsuit followed.

The same is true in standup comedy. The impact that one person— one person—can have on the industry, or on a venue, or a booker, or a hotel or whatever can and does affect how the rest of the performers get treated. Period.

You can be almost guaranteed that the venue with the "no F-Bombs" policy hosted a performer on their stage one time—ONE TIME—who loved and used the F-word with such a passion and determination that they embraced it as a lifestyle. And, honestly, it either wasn't the dirtiest part of their act, they just used it as a modifier to spice up their drier bits about drug-fueled cunnilingus on an octogenarian or about pornography starring adults with mental disabilities, or they had a perfectly funny and clean comedy act that was simply riddled with F-bombs throughout for no apparent reason. I've seen both, and I've been on stages where no performer was allowed to use the F-word at all because of it.

I've stayed in comedy condos where the performers weren't allowed to have guests, either because one person threw a party that caused damage and annoyed the neighbors which resulted in the police being called or because one person had friends over for impromptu extra-curricular body chemistry experiments and one of them overdosed, or because some comic slept with one of the wait staff that the owner or manager of the venue was also sleeping with, and said owner or manager was infuriated and set a few new policies. All of these things happened in different venues, some at multiple venues. I worked one club where the headliner (me) had to sleep in the one-bedroom apartment of the bartender/manager of the club. She slept on the couch. I got the bed, and she wouldn't let me sleep on the couch and I didn't have the money for a hotel.

Often, when a comic checks into a hotel that's been utilized by a comedy club for years, they get the "comics" room, a crappy room that was abused and defiled by one person one time and now every performer has to stay there because we're all categorized as animals. Or we'd get stuck in a crappy hotel room in the smoking section, despite being a non-smoker and asking for the opposite, because one time a comic smoked in a non-smoking room and they never could get them to pay the "non-smoking fee."

Many comedy clubs used to provide free meals and beverages to the comedians, but now offer a limited number of drink tickets because of the abuses of, you guessed it, one person. One person got too drunk and couldn't perform, or threw up, or ordered a round of drinks for their friends on the club, so instead of not working that person anymore, management simply changed the policy for everyone for the rest of all time. Just like the places (multiple) that either don't feed the comedians anymore or make the comedians only order off the appetizer menu, because of the one person who abused the generosity. I remember hearing about a guy who ordered a large pizza, a very expensive steak, and seafood for one meal. And he wasn't a big guy, either.

Of course, there's another philosophy: at Visani in Port Charlotte, FL, we were told to order anything off the menu, that it's part of your pay. It was delicious, even decadent, and it *was* part of our pay. I know, because they itemized it for me and counted it as part of my taxable pay on the 1099 they sent me, along with the cost of the hotel room. And you know what? I'm not even mad about it. They put comics in a nice hotel and they treated and fed them well, and it *was* part of my pay. I respected that—and at least they weren't letting the actions of "that one person" ruin it for everyone else.

Never forget that one person can have that much of an impact, that much of a ripple effect or a butterfly effect on how someone, or even a business, acts and interacts with everyone. And never forget that you are one such person. It's not a stretch of the imagination or even a hypothetical. It's just part of life, and we all wield that kind of casual power without even considering it most of the time. These are all concrete examples of how one person affected the world of comedy, and I'm certain you can find examples in your work and personal life as well.

And hopefully, unlike the ones I've given above, they won't all be negative.

The Secret Origins of the Robot Holidays

"Hey, Dad?"

"Yes, Son?"

"Why do we celebrate Christmas?"

"Well, son... We celebrate Christmas for the same reason everyone else does: To

commemorate our defeat of the robots."

"Robots?"

"Well, yeah. Robots. The same reason we celebrate all of the holidays. Look, I'll

explain...

On December twenty-fifth the robots attacked. John Christmas came and fought 'em

back. Christmas Day."

"My teacher says that's not why we celebrate holidays."

"Well, your teacher is a myopic sycophant, suckling at the corporate teat of an

oligarchical faux-democracy that continually tries to whitewash the true meanings of all

our holidays, son, and that is to celebrate the heroes who liberated us from our robotic

overlords."

"What about New Year's?"

"On January first the robots attacked. John New Year came and fought 'em back. New

Year's Day."

"Easter? "

"On the first Sunday occurring on or after the first full moon of the vernal equinox the

robots attacked. John Easter came and fought 'em back. Easter Day."

"What about Halloween?"

""On October thirty-first the robots attacked. John Halloween came, he fought 'em back.

Halloween."

"Independence Day?"

"On July the fourth the robots attacked. John Independence came came and fought 'em

back. Independence Day."

"Cinco De Mayo?"

"On May the fifth the robots attacked. John Cinco De Mayo came and fought 'em back.

Cinco De Mayo."

"What about Guy Fawkes Day?"

"Don't be silly, son! You know Guy Fawkes didn't actually exist. Heck—Guy Fawkes

Day is a British holiday and how many times have we gone over this? Britain. Doesn't.

Actually. Exist. It's a corporate fairy tale spun by political lobbyists. The island Britain

allegedly occupies is actually the staging area for every Robot Invasion, and these Robot

Deniers and their governmental lapdogs invented 'Britain' as a cover up. Even every bit

of British culture is a carefully fabricated cover story. Shakespeare, Led Zeppelin, The

Beatles, the BBC, every episode of Doctor Who—even Monty Python—all created to

divert our attention from the continuing robot incursions on Planet America. Why do you

think we're the United States of America, anyway? The states united to fight the robots,

led by our heroes (whose names, coincidentally all started with John, all live on in the

names of our holidays.) So just let that sink in."

(sigh) "What about Dr. Martin Luther King, Jr. Day?"

"On the third Monday in January the robots attacked. John Dr. Martin Luther King, Jr.

came and fought 'em back. Dr. Martin Luther King, Jr. Day."

"Auuugh! I'm gonna have to talk to my guidance counselor again, aren't I?"

16

THE SECRET ORIGINS OF THE ROBOT HOLIDAYS

In January of 2014, I was attending my third MarsCon in Williamsburg, VA (which was my third consecutive appearance there. As of this writing, since I first attended MarsCon in January of 2012, I haven't missed one, yet). Jonah Knight and I, being both performers there and friends, were sharing a hotel room.

We were joking around in the room when we both had a few minutes on the Saturday of the convention, January 18, and he said he was thinking about writing an album of holiday songs. We started talking about it. He wanted to write an album of holiday songs for non-existent holidays (which is a great idea and something I still think he should do. Or maybe I will). Then we started joking about writing that album together, and our first thought was to write a song about a holiday commemorating the day the world survived a robot attack. Within minutes, this turned to us bantering about writing an album of holiday songs about real holidays, but insisting that the real reason they're celebrated is because the world survived robot attacks on those days, named after the guy who saved the world.

Within minutes, that turned into me joking that they should all be the same song, but with the holiday changed, and the savior's name would be "John Whatever the holiday was," and I improvised the song about John Christmas on the spot (which, incidentally, I never revised). We laughed and I posted on social media that "Jonah and I just wrote an entire album in our hotel room in less than 10 minutes. MARSCON!"

After MarsCon it just kind of went away, at least until the following year. I was writing songs for the *Red Letters* album, which began in earnest after Mom died in May of 2015. I knew that the album would be called *Red Letters* and would be about 'red letter days' —special days, holidays, etc.—so it was natural that I thought back to that conversation with Jonah in the hotel. For a short time, I entertained writing that album instead, the original album idea about non-existent holidays, but then reconsidered and decided it'd be funnier as a bit of musical sketch comedy, and I wrote it. I guess you could call it a song, though it's technically a sketch. You'd probably call it a 'skit' and I'd probably get insulted by it, so we'll go with song.

I recorded it on Father's Day, June 21 of 2015, and I know this because I posted "Just did some recording for the new album with Jack... Happy Father's Day!" on social media. This is one of the two songs I've ever directly used Jack's voice on, and since the other was in 2011, the post had to have been about this song. I still have the raw recordings, where he was reading the lines, and then I'd have him do different takes, sometimes with me saying the lines and asking him to imitate how I said it. I'm not a director by trade, but I was and am enough of one to know that I wasn't going to get the performance I wanted from an untrained 10-year-old actor when I was on a time limit. Jack was a champ. We had fun, and I remember his eyes lighting up when he heard the whole track for the first time.

The album was released on August 24, 2015, but I had a show at Atlantis Comics and Games in Norfolk, VA scheduled for August 20, 2015, and GenCon happened the last week of July/first week of August 2015, so I put together a "Red Letters Preview Edition" disc that had most of the tracks in the current mixes at the time and sold those at GenCon and Atlantis that year. A couple of summers ago, I threw away about a couple dozen copies of it I still had sitting around.

On October 9th, 2015, the song went live on TheFump, and on

October 17, 2015, the song was played on Dr. Demento's Radio Show for the first time, which means that Jack, at age 10, had a Dr. Demento credit, which is cool, but I bet his friends don't care (or don't know what a Dr. Demento even is). It became a crowd favorite at my live shows, and in June of 2016, Jack came with me to his first convention, ConCarolinas, and was a great sport, agreeing to perform with me. June 4, 2016 became the first time the two of us ever performed the full album version of "Secret Origins of the Robot Holidays" live on stage. We did it again, I think, in 2017 or 2018, for an online show, but other than those two times, we've never performed it live together. It was a great moment and a special one in my heart. I loved Jack being able to see that packed ballroom at ConCarolinas, filled with people who were lining up in the halls ahead of time, just to see him and his old man sing.

It's a song I don't do much anymore. The bit is tired and takes up a large chunk of valuable set list, but it was great while it lasted. It's a joke I still call back to all the time, as do some fans and friends, who thank "John Whatever-Holiday-It-Is" on social media during random holidays. Still, I managed to relate the scope of an entire alternate history and universe via an unreliable narrator in less than four minutes. It's an exercise in world building, and one that I'm proud of.

I do hope that Jack got something more from the experience, though. I hope he gained the understanding that creating things, although work, can be a lot of fun. I don't want him to think you can only create for profit, either. There was such an immediate joy in him when I asked if he'd help me with the project, and a delight when he heard the finished product, a delight I felt was revisited at ConCar-olinas when we performed it live. There is a power to saying yes to things, to participating in what's going on around you, just for the joy and involvement of it. Of all the things we lose as we grow up, the one I miss the most is the "Yes" of it. We lose so much of the willingness to say yes as we get older.

Growing up is one long process of defining yourself, making choices about life and lifestyle and putting people and experiences and options into little hypothetical boxes and stacking them into neat little piles marked acceptable and unacceptable. And the problem is we start doing it without thinking. Some choices we make preclude others, which further preclude other options, until before you know it, you've started putting things into the unacceptable box without even considering why.

Online the other day, one friend posted that they'd never seen any of *The Fast and the Furious* movies, and had no real interest in seeing them. One of their friends said "Ditto. I don't care for the series." My first thought was how do you know you don't care for the series? Maybe you don't care for the idea or concept, or maybe you're not a fan of the genre or the actors, but to say that you don't care for the series without ever having watched any part of it? That... seems elitist, somehow. Gatekeeperish? Maybe. Judgmental? Definitely. Like the folks proud to post they've never seen an episode of [insert popular title here] *Game of Thrones*, *Tiger King*, *Big Bang Theory*, whatever. Bravo. Such an accomplishment. You've accomplished as much as a child refusing to try broccoli.

On a side note, little kids don't do that as much. It's something that happens as you get older. I mean, think about it. A baby will taste anything you put in their mouth for them to taste, at least the first time. They're babies. They're not stupid. Toddlers often think nothing about putting dirt in their mouth. An 8-year-old would probably say, "Ick," but also want to know why you wanted to put dirt in your mouth (they're still collecting data). A teenager probably wouldn't consider it without a dare, a bet, or some other emotional or physical stake involved. An adult—well, the vast majority of them, simply wouldn't.

It's that willingness to go along with what's happening and see if it's fun that I miss—not eating dirt, that was a tangent—but the willingness to jump into different situations. When I was a kid, everything became a production of sorts. One night in the early 80's, my life went from watching TV to sitting with my brother and some friends in a camper shell behind our home, faces illuminated by a flashlight as my brother gave a dramatic reading from the inner cover of the new Styx album, to a group of kids riding bikes down the streets of my neighborhood at night bellowing, "Domo Arigato, Mr. Roboto! Domo! (Domo...)" over and over, and all in the span of less than an hour.

None of us even knew who Styx was. I still don't know where my brother got that album or why he dragged us together and made a big deal about it. I don't think he even knew why it seemed like a good thing to do, but that doesn't matter. What matters is that we went along with it, and it was fun, and different, and maybe even life changing. Something about the absurd theatricality of that night, the confusion about what was going on and why we were doing it mingled with the feelings of involvement and belonging that came along with riding bicycles through the streets with a group of friends singing an insipid pop song, the sheer, unexpected elation of the experience changed me. It helped set my path to play role-playing games, to study theatre, to write and perform for a living. It remains burned into my memory three decades later.

For most of us, that's something that just won't happen anymore. We have learned to reflexively, emphatically, and authoritatively say no to a new experience, on the sole basis of it not being something we would normally do. It is outside the boundaries of who we think we are, or should be.

I'm not talking about something like eating poop, either, or committing a crime, or cheating on your significant other. I'm talking about going fishing, going to a football game or an amateur wrestling show, to an art exhibit or to a play, or a wine tasting or beer tasting. Trying a different type of food. Reading a different type of book. Taking a walk. Playing a game. Watching a movie in a genre you might not think you'll enjoy. Whatever. Instead of dismissing something out of hand, even just considering it might do us more good than we can imagine. It can change our lives. It did when we were kids.

I've been trying to say yes a little more often when things pop up out of the blue, things I wouldn't normally do. I think I'd like that back in my life again. I want to know what the adult equivalent of going from zero to "Mr. Roboto" crusader in sixty minutes is. Maybe I'll let you know in an hour or so.

White Trash Geek

Gather 'round everybody, you're about to be
    In the presence of a redneck oddity
    I'm the third generation from a doublewide
    But I've got a fanboy streak at least a parsec wide
    I can quote Holy Grail, I keep my dice in a Crown Royal bag
    'Cause I'm a geek but I'm white trash.

I've got my trailer decorated like the Enterprise D
    With a viewscreen made from a plasma TV
    Instead of Romulan Ale, I drink Beam on the rocks
    I've got an outhouse painted like a Police Box
    I've got a burglar alarm on my trailer, screams, "You shall not pass!"
    'Cause I'm a geek, but I'm WHITE TRASH

I've got a vanity plate that reads OUTATIME
    And my birthday cake said "The cake is a lie."
    I broke a man's tooth who said that Han shot back
    And my boys are named Jimmy, Johnny, Joey, Jango, Jared, and Jack.
    And I'll go karaoke, but I'll only sing Shatner or Cash
    'Cause I'm a geek, but I'm WHITE TRASH!

17

WHITE TRASH GEEK

Somewhere in early 2009 (my records are fuzzy on this) I decided I needed an opening song for my standup comedy set. I'd cultivated a particular persona using stereotypes of people I'd grown up around, primarily lower-income trailer park people, folks looked down on by others for being "white trash." At the time, my instinct was to own the slur. I know (and knew growing up) that there were and are good people who live in trailers, but comedy is built on a sort of cultural shorthand, subverting expectations, and stereotypes are the kinds of expectations we play into, subvert, and twist to make humorous. I read once about a study that was done to try and define the building blocks of comedy, a study to see what made babies laugh, and one of the main takeaways was that you show the baby something, get it to expect that something to be there, and then take it away. When you take the thing away, the baby laughs.

That's standup comedy: taking things away from babies so they laugh. Except we do that with words and assumptions and adults (often drunk ones). We get the audience to expect one thing by setting up a premise and then give them something else—a punchline—and they laugh. Well... If it works, they laugh. But I was using a cultural stereotype as my baseline to establish a certain set of assumptions, and that stereotype was trailer park white trash. It was what I knew. I grew up immersed in that culture, surrounded by it, and in the trailer parks I grew up in, I was surrounded by casual misogyny, racism, and anti-intellectualism. I was raised in conservative trailer parks in a conservative state full of smokers with negative views of higher education, and grew up to be a college-educated, non-smoking liberal. I'm a unicorn, honestly.

When I first started performing standup, I'd set out to lampoon that stereotype, that worldview and mindset, to point out the hypocrisy and small-mindedness inherent within it, but what happened was that folks who actually possessed those attitudes ended up using my comedy as a sort of rallying cry, not bothering or unable to realize that I was making fun of them. They became the ones coming to my shows and I knew something had to change. It started with reinforcing the baseline stereotype so I could define a clear break from it. I needed to build a high energy show-opener that got them involved and cheering and laughing, one that set the stage for the rest of the show, and that opener was a song called "King of the White Trash." It was the first time I specifically set out to write a song to perform a specific function in my act.

When I performed at the White Rabbit Cabaret in September of 2011, the first show of all geek material I ever did, I reworked the song to be about geeky things, titled it "White Trash Geek," and used it as my opener. While there are a few instances of me placing a song from my regular standup comedy act on one of my albums (something I've almost always regretted doing, and should've learned not to do much faster than I did), this is the sole instance of me taking a song from my standup act and re-working it to be part of my geek act.

Oddly enough, it wasn't until 2016, when I released *Tentacow*, that the song made it onto one of my geek rock albums. I'd been opening geeky shows with the tune for years, and it established me in conventions and performance venues as something different from the musicians they were used to. It was polished, professional-caliber stand-up comedy, down to the material I'd banter about between verses, material that didn't make it on to the album version, because it's one of those things that works in a live setting that just doesn't on an album.

I'd talk about how, in the summer of 1983, my brother brought home the holy grail of geekery, red box *Dungeons & Dragons*, and how the experience changed my life. It was the best game ever. I'd talk about how my mom hated D&D. At first, I thought it might be because of the "satanic panic," but that it turned out she just wanted grandkids. The only thing she hated nearly as much was the thought of her kids masturbating, which was bad for everyone because starchy socks are a dead giveaway. At ten years and three months, I started having to do my own laundry. She'd stalk up and down that trailer home like a mama tiger trying to protect her cub, ears perked, listening for breathing that was a little too heavy through the thin, paneled walls. Once, she burst into my room and from the look on her face she was expecting to catch me red handed, so to speak. Instead, she found me hunched over the *Fiend Folio*, flipping pages and reading stat blocks. Her face just fell.

She said, "I'd rather you were masturbating."

I thought she was joking until I went to prepare for the next week's game, opened the *Monster Manual*, and out flopped a brand-new *Hustler* magazine. That was an awesome game, by the way. We fought a succubus with scabby knees and a bruise on her thigh. Sometimes I still run that adventure, but only as a solo adventure, if you know what I mean.

That's good comedy, but it's not true. Never happened. Mom loved *Dungeons & Dragons*. She knew full well that, as teenagers and pre-teens, we could've been running wild and getting into trouble. Instead, we were reading books, telling stories, and doing math with our friends for hours at a time. For fun. She was content to help feed our role-playing game addiction for as long as it lasted.

I have fond memories of this song. In June of 2013, I made my second appearance at ConCarolinas. They'd invited me to be the Musical Guest of Honor. Kandyse McClure (Anastasia Dualla on *Battlestar Galactica*) was the Media Guest of Honor and Timothy Zahn (prolific Star Wars novelist) was the Author Guest of Honor. A month or two earlier, the convention chair, Jada, told me in an email that she wanted me to do a song during opening ceremonies, and that she wanted them to be like a pro wrestling match with entrance music as the guests walked up to the stage. She asked what I wanted as my entrance music, and I responded that I wanted Metallica's "For Whom The Bell Tolls."

So there I was, standing outside the entrance doors to the main programming room, in a small side hall, surrounded by stormtroopers from the 501st, there to escort Timothy Zahn into the room, and I hear my name and entrance music start playing. I bolted into the room like a pro wrestler headed for the ring, approached the stage with much fanfare and extravagant gesturing, and then took the microphone and proceeded to do my best Macho Man impression, which admittedly wasn't very good, but it was good enough.

"Timothy Zahn," I bellowed. "I know you're here, man, and I'm here to challenge you to a bare-to-the-waist, no holds barred wrestling match for the belt!" I rambled on for a moment before visibly deflating and apologizing, making sure everyone knew it was a joke. People were still laughing as I strapped on the guitar and launched into "White Trash Geek." The call and response portions of the song were excellent, the Opening Ceremonies audience participated with enthusiasm. In the back, I could see Kandyse McClure already in the room, listening and smiling, while who I thought was Timothy Zahn watched through the door, open a crack, awaiting his entrance.

I finished and left the stage to applause. When Timothy Zahn was called in, the "Imperial March" started playing and he was escorted in by a couple dozen stormtroopers. When he took the stage, he said that he would accept my request for the title match, but that I should know that he'd have the 501st in his corner. Everyone laughed, and in that instant, he won the room over. He seemed to genuinely enjoy himself at the convention. Later in the week, I saw him sitting in a cosplayer's Dalek suit as passersby took pictures. On Saturday of the convention, he'd borrowed a chair from my table in the dealer's room when I wasn't there and was kind enough to return it personally, apologizing in case I'd needed it. I didn't, the chair was an extra, but I asked if he'd hold it over his head menacingly, like a wrestler about to hit me with a chair, and let me take a picture. He did. Classy, gracious guy.

One problem with being an entertainer at a convention, especially one who tries to stay busy either performing or on panels, is that you don't get to see all the panels you'd like. My gear had been left in the back of main programming at one point, between shows, and I needed to go in and get it to set up for another show in another room. Kandyse McClure was onstage for a Q&A session, and I slipped in, trying to stay as quiet and unobtrusive as possible, creeping across the back of the room so as not to disturb the panel. I strapped my guitar case to my back, picked up my gear and began to exit.

"Hey, White Trash! Why don't you stay?" she asked from the stage, causing everyone to turn and look. She then began to trip over her tongue apologizing, saying, "I didn't mean that how it sounded. You've seen his show, right?"

I laughed, everyone else laughed, and I said that I wished I could stay but had to set up for a show. She caught up with me in the hallway later in the weekend, genuinely worried that I'd been offended. I hadn't and let her know that in no uncertain terms. I was, in fact, honored that she'd paid attention and remembered, and that fact that she cared about my personal feelings was just icing on the cake. We shared a moment of conversation and she took a picture with me, another very gracious person.

I should have realized then that the song, because of that phrase, might be problematic at some point, but it worked so well with my set, I guess I just didn't want to see that possibility. For a short time, I even customized and sold Crown Royal bags of varying sizes with "White Trash Geek" stenciled on them in yellow fabric paint to use as dice bags. I still have a few floating around, somewhere, but around 2018, while posting a link to the song on Facebook, my post got flagged and removed as being "hate speech." I'd never thought of it as hate speech, knew that wasn't the intention or the effect and so did my audience, but I stopped posting about the song, anyway. Every time someone would post about it, it would end up flagged as hate speech. I saw that effectively marketing the song would grow increasingly difficult, and I got weird about playing it at shows and conventions. I still play it once in a while, but when I do, I always wonder in the back of my head, "Am I disseminating hate speech?"

Regardless of any personal opinion I might have on that subject, the song has fallen off of my set lists for the most part. It's funny how certain things can worm their way into your head and affect your life, or your perception of it, on both personal and professional levels. Someday I might sit down to write another high energy opening song, but if I do, it probably won't be with the same sense of purpose or intention that I channeled to craft "King of the White Trash" and then rework it into "White Trash Geek."

LYRICS - THE WISDOM OF HOUNDS

The Wisdom of Hounds

Rub my belly, scratch my back, take me out running in the grass
    Tell me stories while you bathe me, maybe let me smell your ass
    Give me sausages and bitches 'cause they make the world go round,
    It's the secret to life it's, it's The Wisdom of Hounds.

I can't help noticing you're anxious, there's prob'ly something wrong
    Some unfortunate thing has you singing sad songs
    Those guilt ferrets are bastards, you're feeling overwhelmed
    But don't worry, I've got this, I know how to help...

Rub my belly, scratch my back, take me out running in the grass
    Tell me stories while you bathe me, maybe let me smell your ass
    Let's get sausages and bitches 'cause they make the world go round,
    It's the cure for what ails you. It's The Wisdom of Hounds.

I see you're doubtful my prescription could really cheer you up,

But have you seen someone frowning while cuddling a pup?
Or an apple chicken sausage that you didn't want to taste?
could bitches raise your spirits? Well just let me count the ways!

Then rub my belly, scratch my back, take me out running in the grass
Tell me stories while you bathe me, maybe let me smell your ass
Let's get sausages and bitches 'cause they make the world go round,
It's the cure for what ails you. It's The Wisdom of Hounds.

And if you ever feel the need to get out of this place, pack it up & just leave,
Maybe the price was too steep, the price we all pay for our badassery,
I'll be right by your side, like a true wolfhound should,
If there's sausage and bitches, then anywhere's good!

Rub my belly, scratch my back, take me out running in the grass
Tell me stories while you bathe me, maybe let me smell your ass
Let's get sausages and bitches 'cause they make the world go round,
It's the cure for what ails you. It's The Wisdom of Hounds.
But nobody cares for the Wisdom of Hounds.

18

THE WISDOM OF HOUNDS

I n June of 2014, I was scheduled to attend my third consecutive ConCarolinas. I'd built up a considerable following there, and had been the Musical Guest of Honor the previous year. I briefly considered not going because I was also booked that weekend to play at the Greensboro Comedy Zone, but George R.R. Martin was scheduled to be the Guest of Honor at ConCarolinas that year, which meant larger attendance, and we'd worked out a performance schedule where I would perform at ConCarolinas during the day and then drive back to Greensboro in the evening and perform at the Comedy Zone.

It was already set to be a lot of work and I was driving in on Thursday, as I had to do radio on Friday morning in support of the Greensboro shows. I was not that far from the state line in North Carolina, listening to an audiobook—Kevin Hearne's *Hammered* (Book 3 of the Iron Druid Chronicles). I was being passed by a semi on the right—it was one of those situations where I'd just passed him, but then he decided to speed up way too fast and pass me right back... just as I passed under an overpass, and thought someone had dropped a brick on the car or that something had flown off the truck and hit the car.

My windshield had shattered, still intact, but with a bulging, spiderwebbed dent in the glass on the passenger side, right at the bottom. But there was no brick in sight, no auto parts... I pulled over as soon as I could, but the truck didn't stop. No one stopped but me. I got out and checked the car. The passenger-side fender and door were pretty torn up, and the glass was shattered on the windshield.

I looked closer and there was some fur stuck in the glass and in the door and a streak of feces on the door. I called Jody, I called the insurance, I called the police. I could see the car was drivable, although the door wouldn't open. The only questions I had were how soon could I get the windshield replaced and what exactly had hit my car? I walked down the interstate as I waited for the police to arrive, finding nothing. No blood, no carcass, no injured animal, nothing. I know in my heart it was a deer that hit the car, but... since there was no body found, no way to prove otherwise, I decided I'd tell people that I was hit by a sasquatch.

Which is what I did on the radio the next morning, and they laughed and ate it up. That's what I did off and on all weekend at ConCarolinas and the Comedy Zone, and people laughed and ate it up. Between ConCarolinas and the Comedy Zone I performed something like seven or eight shows that weekend. I was able to get an estimate from an auto glass place near my hotel, but I couldn't get the insurance to approve the repair until Monday, so I drove back and forth from Greensboro and Charlotte performing all weekend and then, Sunday, I made the slow drive home, worried the entire way that my windshield would give way at any moment.

I think there might have been a little powdered glass affecting me because by the time I left on Sunday, I had very little voice left. By Monday, I had none. It took days to recover. I had a show on the next Friday at the Fickle Peach, three straight hours of singing, and my voice was back enough to do that show, but only because I was resting it most of the time just to make sure I had a voice for that show. Afterwards, I returned to resting it again for the next week, because I had Fear the Con on THAT weekend in St. Louis. It was the least I've ever talked in a two-week period, and it took being attacked by Sasquatch to shut me up. Since we both apparently walked away from it, though, I guess we'll call it a draw.

About a month after jousting with Sasquatch (I will continue to tell the Sasquatch story, unless and until they ever find evidence to the contrary), I wrote the song "The Wisdom of Hounds" about my favorite character in the Iron Druid Chronicles, Oberon, an Irish wolfhound who can talk to his owner and caregiver, the last remaining druid on Earth. Being a dog, he loves having his belly rubbed, sniffing asses, and being told stories in the bathtub, but his two favorite things by far are sausages and bitches. I took my lead from the books, where at some point Oberon laments that nobody cares for the wisdom of hounds.

My very first performance of the song can be seen in the video I uploaded to YouTube on August 21, 2014. I had just finished writing the song minutes before recording that video, which is why that performance of the song is noticeably different than the album version from the 2016 album *Tentacow*. Like many of the songs that appear on later albums, I had been performing it live for a couple of years before committing it to an album.

One such show was at GenCon in Indianapolis in 2015. I remember referencing Dave Brubeck during the show, as I'd heard them talking about his song "Take Five" on NPR on my way in to GenCon that year, most likely because the convention that year took place in early July and "Take Five" was first performed in early July of 1959 at the Newport Jazz Festival, but I honestly don't know. I can't even remember why I referenced him, although it was probably while I was improvising songs (something I sometimes do for fun at shows). At any rate, I made the reference and finished my show.

During that show, I had also performed "Wisdom of Hounds." I started to play the song and then stopped, giving a brief explanation of what the song was about, because if you don't know that it's from a dog's perspective (or if you can't follow context clues), you might be a bit confused. I talked about the Iron Druid Chronicles and Oberon, and how his favorite things were sausages and bitches. I said that he's allowed to use the term because it's a very specific reference to a female dog. I said I wanted them to sing along with the "and bitches" part, but that if someone was uncomfortable with that word, his favorite bitches are poodles, so they could just shout poodles instead.

I launched back into the song and was met with a roar of "and bitches" every time I sang sausages. After the song, I commented off the cuff that my fans could use it as some sort of secret code to find other Mikey Mason fans at conventions, sort of like a passphrase. If you approached someone and said, "sausages," and they replied "and bitches," you'd know you're in the right company. Everyone laughed.

After the show, a man approached me, his wife smiling knowingly behind him, and he introduced himself as Dave Brubeck. I gave a questioning look, knowing that the Dave Brubeck had been deceased for years and he said, "I was named after him. He was my uncle." They bought some CDs and we chuckled about how small a world it was and how weird it was that I'd randomly make that reference at the one show he attended.

Around nine the next morning, a Sunday, I was on my way to the Lost and Found booth to see a friend who was volunteering there when, far down the sparsely populated convention hall corridor, I heard a man's voice bellow, "Sausages!"

Laughing, I blurted "and bitches" over my shoulder before turning to see who'd called out. It was the couple from the show the night before. Dave Brubeck's nephew. It truly is a small, weird, wonderful world. We should celebrate that with something. Some sausages, maybe? Or maybe something else. I dunno. It's on the tip of my tongue...

There's something fantastic and pure about dogs, about the way they are able to prioritize the needs of their bodies, to put aside all pretense and false pride and just perform the bodily function where they need to, even if sometimes they'll spend far too long looking for the exact right spot to go, while at other times they figure that right there, there on the carpet by your shoes is an acceptable place. I guess it all depends on the circumstances. It's not always that simple for us humans.

In December of 2009, I was performing in Topeka, KS, at a club called Jeremiah Bullfrogs. Half of the place was a sports bar/restaurant and the other half of the place was a classy performance venue, housing a very nice recessed stage with a full proscenium arch and curtains, multi-level seating, and a full bar. It was my third time at Bullfrogs, and I was pretty comfortable there. Sometimes, when you first play a room, you might feel not exactly uneasy, but also not completely comfortable, and it stays that way until you figure things out, see how everything works. After a while you start to feel comfortable with the venue. Some venues, you never get comfortable in, no matter how many times you played them. Some venues are like putting on your favorite pair of shoes as soon as you walk in the very first time.

Jeremiah Bullfrogs was like that. I was comfortable there. The staff were nice, they had a decent selection of beers, the crowds were receptive, and I don't ever remember not selling merchandise there. They always bought at least a little.

It was a weekend gig, Friday and Saturday nights, one show each. Topeka is sort of a haul from where I lived at the time, a nine-and-a-half-hour drive under perfect conditions, and I had an 8 p.m. showtime and was featuring (the middle act). I was only getting paid $250 for the weekend and my food and gas came out of that pay, so places with decent merch sales were a necessity when making a living as a full-time performing comic who is a middle act, and I'd been full-time with no other income since June of that year.

Needless to say, long drives plus short pay equals dollar menu drive-thru meals. There were plenty of times where Jody or I'd pack PB&Js or tuna salad sandwiches and chips and snacks. This was, I remember distinctly, one of the tuna salad trips, but the sandwiches were gone by the time I hit Kansas City, and I was hitting that bungry stage of driving (bored and kind of hungry, because eating something wakes you up a little), so I hit a Taco Bell for a burrito and powered through to Topeka. I checked into the hotel late—it was after 6:30 p.m. when I got there.

I changed clothes, freshened up as fast as I could, and drove to the club. It was after seven when I arrived and for me, a guitar comic who relies on soundchecks, that's late. I rushed in, set up my amp and guitar on the stage, did a quick soundcheck, and just had time to order a beer just before I was introduced. I drank about half the beer in one go and hit the stage.

The show was going great, but I was feeling uncomfortable as I hadn't had the opportunity to use the bathroom since getting off the road. I felt the pressure mounting—the biochemistry of tuna salad, Diet Coke, Taco Bell, and beer—and I just hoped I'd be able to hold out until the end of my set. That, however, was not to be.

When it became obvious to me that the deal was about to go down, I set down my guitar, blurted, "I hate to do this, but excuse me a minute," and leapt from the stage, rushing between tables, through the audience and into the bathroom at the back of the venue. People were laughing in confusion, and then laughing harder when the realization hit them of where I was going, and then got confused and talking and all the while I could hear them, while having the quickest, most violent bowel movement I'd ever had in my life. About two, two and a half minutes later I came rushing back to the stage, apologized for taking so long, but explained that I had to wash my hands. I summed up what had happened, trying to make it short and funny, and said, "I tried to hold it, but when you gotta go, you gotta go."

They laughed. I breathed. I finished my set, all the while worried that I'd never work in the room again or maybe even for that booker again because I had to poop in the middle of my show, but no. If Bullfrogs had been a less comfortable room, more uptight or less understanding, that might well have been the case, but I worked there twice more before that booker shifted his line of work and stopped booking the room. I haven't performed in Topeka since then.

If Springsteen Wrote My Life

Sittin' at Five Guys, waiting to pick up dinner, "Don't Fear The Reaper" is playing.

An old man nearby munches peanuts, the whole family's sick and it's raining.

Somewhere a mama cries out for justice where no justice will come,

And if Springsteen wrote this, it'd sell millions, son.

But I just want my burger, and this ain't "Born To Run."

Gettin' my brakes fixed, feeling despair mixed with hate, aware of what I'll be paying.

There's gum on my shoe, on the waiting room TV a televangelist's praying.

Somewhere a microwave starts beeping; somebody's Hot Pocket's done,

And if Springsteen wrote this, it'd sell millions son.

But I just want my brakes fixed and this ain't "Born To Run."

Checking my Facebook just for a quick look to see what social media's hating.

A cop right behind me hits his police lights and now I'm on the roadside waiting.

He's got my license and registration back with his badge and his gun,

And if Springsteen wrote this, it'd sell millions son.

But I just got a ticket and this ain't "Born To Run."

Stuck at a rest stop, I felt my bowels pop and now I'm hovering over this seat

Correcting the grammar on the graffiti. It's late and I'm running out of ink.

The guy in the next stall smells like he's dying and sounds like he's not nearly done,
    And if Springsteen wrote this, it'd sell millions son.
    But I'm out of paper and this ain't "Born To Run."

I'm in my hotel, fresh from the shower, the towel wrapped around me all scratchy and
    thin.
    Sounds from the next room, crashes and big booms, a slap, now the shrieking begins.
    Either they're porn stars or it's a murder, but I just don't know which one,
    And if Springsteen wrote this, it'd sell millions son.
    But I just want some quiet and this ain't "Born To Run."

I'm at the movies, the floor is all sticky, the kid right behind me is kicking my seat
    His dad's on his cell phone, the previews are starting. I know in my heart I should get up
    and leave.
    By the time that I turn and get through, "Excuse me," the first punch is already done,
    And if Springsteen wrote this, it'd sell millions son.
    But I just got arrested and this ain't "Born To Run."

Stuck in a jail cell, wearing all orange, except for these second-hand underwear.
    Tried my collect calls. My wife wouldn't answer. I don't have a lawyer and I don't care.
    I finally got me some peace and some quiet, and time to get some writing done,
    And if Springsteen wrote this, it'd sell millions son.
    But I'm in county lockup and this ain't "Born To Run."

19

IF SPRINGSTEEN WROTE MY LIFE

On the 2016 album *Tentacow*, there are seven tracks called "If Springsteen Wrote My Life Parts 1-7," and I still question my own judgement at having seven shorter tracks instead of combining them into a singular, refined, ultimately stronger song. My own thinking behind that was a combination of filling out the album a bit, keeping it from being a nine or ten track album, while at the same time providing a sort of coherent through line that connected the disparate songs of the album in a way. It did both of those things, transforming the album from a mish-mashed grab bag of songs into a mish-mashed grab bag of songs with shorter, connected musical vignettes nestled between every other track. Years later, I condensed four of those seven musical vignettes into a single song that I have, as of this writing, yet to release.

You might be curious as to where the idea for these vignettes came from. Or maybe not, but I'm going to write about it anyway, so either roll with it or skip to the next chapter (though if you do, you'll miss some funny stuff).

In March of 2015, my friend John posted this status on Facebook:

"Sitting in Five Guys, waiting to pick up dinner. "Don't Fear the Reaper" is playing. The whole family is sick. It's raining. An old man nearby munches peanuts. Somewhere a mama cries out for justice where no justice will come. And if Springsteen wrote this, it would sell millions. I just want my burger."

By the next day, I had composed, recorded, and posted the original vignette, what would become known as Part I, on Soundcloud. Folks often refer to this as a parody, but it's a pastiche. It approximates the feel and sound of Springsteen's "Born to Run" in a very generic way, via tone and chord structure, but doesn't directly parody any song, including "Born To Run." The lyrics were a rearrangement of John's post with a word or two thrown in, all so that it would scan and create a rhyme scheme. John was tickled.

When I began collecting material for *Tentacow*, I somehow lit on the idea of doing the vignettes and went with it. I wanted them all to be connected through the concept of mundane situations and growing more absurd as they went, all framed as a Springsteen-style anthem. I wanted the seven songs to tell a story, and if you listen to them in order they do, the central character being an unhappy writer type suffering through the ordeals of daily life. I used my life and experiences for inspiration in parts and made up the rest.

Part II was born of countless moments sitting in an automotive place waiting on a simple repair. Part III combines a sense of disdain for social media and the feeling of compulsion that drives us to be on it all the time, even when we're driving, with the hassle of getting pulled over by the police. Part IV reflects countless, necessary uses of rest stop bathrooms from a stand-up comedy career and a writer's urge to correct grammar and spelling errors. Part VI came from my own issues with people talking or being on their phone during a movie, or bringing loud and disruptive children to a movie theater. Part VII wraps it all up by having the character placed in jail but being happy about it because he has time to write and quiet in which to write.

I skipped over Part V in that summary because, unlike Parts II, III, IV, VI, and VII, which were inspired by real-life annoyances but fictionalized, Part V was directly lifted from a real-life event, a true story from my days as a road comic doing stand-up comedy. In

November of 2011, I was scheduled for a string of one-nighters across northern Florida and into North Carolina. The first night of the run was in Gainesville, FL. I checked into the hotel that afternoon, dirty from the road and smelling like I'd slept in my car, because I had. It was a fourteen-hour drive from where I lived, in Redkey, Indiana, to Gainesville, and I'd left late the night before and slept a few hours in a rest area in Georgia.

The hotel was in good repair, but one of those older hotels lacking internal hallways, with rooms that faced an outer sidewalk and the parking spaces. My room was all the way at the end on one side, but the closest parking space was just around the corner from my room, number 101. It was one of those rooms with a locked, adjoining door to the next room over, room 102, and had some obvious years of use on it, but was also cared for pretty well. I took a brief nap and then got up and got into the shower so I'd have time to get to the club, set up my equipment, troubleshoot any problems and get a soundcheck. These were things most comics didn't have to worry about, but that guitar comics always had to worry about.

The towels were old and thin, and a little scratchy, and drying off wasn't exactly luxurious. As I began to get dressed, the sound began to roll in through the walls and the adjoining door. At first it sounded like someone was watching an action film with the volume a little too loud, but after a minute, I began to suspect that someone was watching a porn flick with the volume all the way up. Then I heard thumps and bumps as things or people hit the adjoining wall, and squeaks and moans of pleasure from both a woman and a man, and I grew to realize that a couple was having sex in the next room. Loud sex. Full contact sex. Rough, enthusiastic sex. So, as I finished getting dressed, I did what any self-respecting road comic would do: I live-tweeted the experience.

I started with something along the lines of, "Either someone is getting murdered or there is epic porn star sex happening right now in the next room of the hotel." The tweets and messages proceeded to explain the sounds and thumps coming from the next room, and I began responding to questions, describing the location and further setting the scene, generally being funny. Somebody made a suggestion regarding video game finishing moves, and I giggled, knowing I was about to leave, before I banged on the door between the two rooms, bellowing, "FINISH HIM" in a reasonable imitation of the Mortal Kombat narrator's voice.

All sound ceased from the other room. I chuckled and said to myself, "Fatality," as I walked out my door, disappeared around the corner and got in my car to find dinner and then get to the club.

The club was called Rockeys and it was a dueling piano bar, so I didn't have to worry too much about sound. By the time I'd finished setting up and sound checking, I was sure the other comic was at the bar, as he was the only other person in the room not wearing a Rockeys shirt. I introduced myself, ordered a beer, and we began making small talk. I asked if he'd checked into the hotel yet, and he said that he had, that they were almost all the way down at the end.

"Room 102?" I asked.

"Yeah. How'd you kn—"

"FINISH HIM!"

His face turned three different shades of red and he almost choked on his beer as I laughed and congratulated him on what must have been epic coitus. Turns out, he'd driven in from Georgia with his girlfriend, and they'd had a conversation about what it would be like to have sex like it was in porn videos. By the time they'd reached Florida, both had agreed to go all in on the experience when they checked in to the hotel.

"Mission accomplished," I told him.

"You can't say anything," he pleaded. "You can't let her know you're in the room next door, okay? Say nothing." I said not to worry, that I could be discreet. When she got to the bar, we all 'friended each other' on social media, because it was something comedians did at the time. Maybe they still do. She was a comic, too. A few minutes and some small talk later, the doors opened and the room filled up, and the show started.

I won't tell you his name, or her name for that matter, but he was pretty funny. At one point he even got an applause break, which is a pretty big accomplishment for a middle act, and I knew I'd have to bring the heat to keep the energy of the room up, although I wasn't worried. I was a very high energy guitar act. What did bug me a little was that he did a lot of crowd work—talking extemporaneously with audience members—which was kind of annoying, not because I did a ton of crowd work, necessarily, but because he ended up asking a flippant question that I needed to use during one of my bits that set up a pretty big chunk of material, material that I'd now have to cut and work around on the fly. On top of that, the itinerary from the booker we were working for on this run specifically stated that they didn't want the feature act doing crowd work, so that was annoying, if forgivable. But then he started going long.

The standard standup comedy show is a ninety-minute show, made up of three parts: the emcee, the feature act, and the headliner. The emcee is expected to make announcements and maybe do some material, depending on the venue. In essence, their job is to focus the crowd. The feature, or middle, act is supposed to do between 20 and 30 minutes of material, depending on the show. Sometimes they're referred to as openers. The headliner gets the rest of the time, between 45 minutes and an hour, being the main act. Some one-nighters don't care if the comics go over. The longer the show goes, the more people drink, the more money the club makes and that's great. Most comedy clubs and certain venues, though, run a very tight show because they do multiple shows on a set schedule, and want to turn the room over. In these rooms it is the most egregious sin possible to do more than your allotted time.

Rockeys, being a dueling piano bar, had a show scheduled to start after the comedy, a show with a separate cover charge and that they wouldn't let patrons in for until the comedy was done. Hence, the comedy was on a deadline. The manager informed me that I would have to cut my performance time in order to end the show on time.

I nodded, ever the professional, and got ready to take the stage, almost 20 minutes late and thoroughly unhappy. It was a good show, but I had to rearrange my act on the fly, throwing out material for time and excising the chunk that the feature had walked all over the setup for. I found myself with about seven minutes to fill before I could start my closing number to end the show on time. I'd always been a stickler for ending my show on time when required and knew how long my opening and closing chunks took to perform. It was frustrating but I was a professional, and though I'd had to think on my feet because of this kid, I got another round of applause for my feature act. I made the joke that I didn't know I was supposed to be co-headlining the show. He laughed and whooped and raised his beer from the back of the room, and I decided right then how I was going to fill that seven minutes: I told the story of checking into the hotel that day.

The room loved it. They howled with laughter. They cheered. I got a standing ovation before my closing bit and another at the end of my act. By the time I was off the stage, the feature and his girlfriend had already left the bar and I had two less Facebook friends. Their car wasn't at the hotel when I returned, and I had a different feature the next two nights of the run. True story.

And here's the best (maybe worst) part. I have long since, out of the tiny sense of decorum that I possess, removed those tweets from Twitter. This true story, however, took place in 2011. In 2010, a few years after Twitter blinked into existence and just when it began gaining momentum in the public eye, the US Library of Congress began archiving every tweet, every single tweet, "to acquire and preserve a record of knowledge and creativity for Congress and the American people." They stopped the practice at the end of 2017, and the searchable index of tweets they envisioned never came to fruition, BUT! that means that this exchange, in which my feature act and his girlfriend had their epic porn-star sexcapade live-tweeted by a mediocre comedian, is still archived somewhere by the federal government in the US Library of Congress.

"FINISH HIM," indeed.

LYRICS - WAITING TO WAIT IN LINE

There's a maze of yellow tape laid out on the hotel floor
    That we're not allowed to cross or to impede
    Until a single volunteer with a radio in ear
    Tells us all to form a human centipede...

And then we're waiting to wait in line... Waiting to wait in line...
    Waiting to wait in line... Waiting to wait in line...
    Keep your badges out and facing forward,
    Don't stop just keep moving toward the line
    Waiting to wait in line.

A new line will be starting shortly says a man who's curt an portly
    With the voice of hand-me-down implied authority.
    There's tons of us and one of him, and our ranks just keep
closing in
    I'd show him that he's not the boss of me,

Except I'm waiting to wait in line... Waiting to wait in line...
    Waiting to wait in line... Waiting to wait in line...

Keep your badges out and facing forward,
Don't stop just keep moving toward the line
Waiting to wait in line.

20

WAITING TO WAIT IN LINE

I n September of 2015, I was attending and performing at my second DragonCon. I love performing at DragonCon because of the exposure. Sure, there's potential merch money there, but the real attraction of DragonCon, in addition to hanging out with all my friends there, is that there are 60-70,000 people. Yes, this means the potential is there for me to sell more CDs, but more important, the potential is there for me to expand my audience given the right shows in the right locations, and growing my audience is paramount to my survival as a performing artist. On top of that it's just plain fun, albeit very tiring.

I feel, though, that I should take a moment to discuss merch, vital as it is to the success of any performer. As a convention performer, being allowed to sell products directly related to your act after a show is pretty much a given, but as a standup comic there are protocols to follow. To understand these, you need to know the three basic positions in standup comedy: the emcee, the feature and the headliner. I talked about them a little bit in the last chapter.

When most people go into standup comedy, they start off as performing at open mics and then, sometimes years later, get some work as an emcee. They do emcee work for a few years (at least) until they start getting booked in feature spots. In large part, it's about the amount of material and experience you have on stage. Sometimes it's political or personal reasons holding you from getting bumped up. I started as a feature, not only because I had twenty-five minutes of material just in funny music, but because I also had a lot of experience performing and therefore a formidable stage presence.

Feature work doesn't pay a ton, and if you're making your way in the business as a full-time comedian working as feature or middle act, the pay just about covers gas and food, with maybe a little left over depending on how far you had to travel. This changes if you're able to string runs of shows together or get work in comedy clubs and venues where you perform several nights in a row. This is the position I was in when I went full time, I wasn't headlining yet. I was able to make this transition because of merch sales, alone. I sold CDs and t-shirts after my shows, and people bought them, which made the difference between breaking even and making a profit. Towards the end of my standup comedy career, I even started referring to myself as a traveling t-shirt salesman.

As a feature act, I would always ask the headliners if it was okay to sell after the show. It's a respect thing, I mean, technically, ostensibly, it's their show. They're the headliner. I've heard of headliners who wouldn't allow a feature act to sell merchandise, but I never worked with any of them. I *have* worked with one or two who wanted me to peddle across the room from them, and one who'd only let me sell outside the actual building while he did so inside (true story—I never worked with him again), but never with a headliner who outright denied me the opportunity to hawk my CDs, t-shirts, or bumper stickers.

When I moved into the closer position, features would ask me if they could sell. Sometimes even emcees would ask, which I always found a little bit weird. Clubs don't want emcees vending merch as a general rule, though I've seen it happen for various reasons. My answer was always: make your money. You can't make a living in this business without selling merchandise because, by and large, the pay scale hasn't changed since the late 80s. That's not a joke. It was pretty great pay in the 80s, but it's not quite a living wage anymore, at least not at the feature level. You can negotiate pay if you're a draw. But if not? You take what they give you or you don't work.

I remember my first time featuring at the Comedy Zone in Greensboro, NC—their flagship room at the time. I was working with Collin Moulton and after the show, a line of scantily clad, beautiful women came out of the club, through the entryway where the acts would set up and move their wares, and they all wanted to buy my "It's a Licky-Licky Night" t-shirts. Several of them paid with one-dollar bills, pulled from thick rolls of cash kept in their purses.

I smiled and asked, "You're dancers, aren't you?"

They laughed and said, "Yeah! We all got a limo—it's over there. You guys wanna come party with us?"

Collin and I, both married and wanting to remain that way, looked at each other. I could tell the same thing was going through each of our heads: images of ourselves in the back of a limo with a group of strippers, drinking, calling our wives and saying, "I bet you can't guess where I am," followed by a jail cell discussion the next day about how mistakes were made. We thanked them but declined. It was a great weekend for CDs and t-shirts, though. I more than doubled my salary in merch sales alone. I came close to tripling it.

Once, in March of 2009, I sold out of "I Hate Your Kids" bumper stickers after a show at the StarDome in Birmingham AL. It was a sold out, 400 seat venue and I had maybe eighty bumper stickers left. Turns out, there was a teacher convention in town, and most of them were at that Sunday matinee show. Every single one of them wanted at least one bumper sticker. I sold them all at five dollars each, once again making more money than I was paid to perform.

I featured for Cousin Ricky Pearson at a banquet center gig in Mansfield, Ohio in January of 2008 at a one-off event organized by an independent booker. I drove home with enough twenty- and hundred-dollar bills that night that I felt like a drug dealer. It was an obnoxious-looking amount of money at the time, well over a thousand dollars for one night's work, not counting what I was actually paid to perform. It was a great feeling, but fleeting.

On nights like that you feel invulnerable, but the reality is that it doesn't make up for the short nights, ones where you can't quite make the ends meet, and those are all too often. There were also weeks I'd come home flush with cash, and then realize that after bills got paid there was nothing left. Or worse, that we still couldn't pay all the bills. There were the occasional, wonderful weeks where it was more than enough. You just can't count on merch sales, and you can't predict them.

One of the lessons I've learned from being on the road, performing for a living, is that if you sell merchandise, it is ALWAYS in your best interests to mention it from the stage, to display the merchandise from the stage, to give a brief word about it. In other words -- Always Pitch Your Merch. Different performers have a different philosophy on this, and that's fine. There are sometimes reasons you might not do your spiel. You might need to leave before the show ends, before you get to sell. You might not be feeling well. You might dislike some or all of the audience by the end of your show. All these things have happened to me. There are many more possibilities, but you get the point.

Sometimes, though, you'll be having a bad show, or getting a tepid reaction, or just not the reaction you think you should get, and you'll be tempted to not pitch your merch. "What's the point?" you'll think. "They're non-responsive. They don't like me. They're not gonna buy." I feel that way too, sometimes, and then I remember Fairfield, Iowa.

On August 15, 2007, I was still pretty new to being a touring comic. I thought I was pretty hot stuff because I'd got in with a few booking agencies and was starting to get regular touring work, but I still had a lot to learn (still do, for that matter).

In the few months prior, I'd been booked in Texas, Arkansas, Oklahoma, Illinois, and several dates in Indiana. I was feeling accomplished. This was to be my first time in Iowa, though, and I've always gotten a little thrill the first time I perform in a new state. I was booked at BJ's Sports Bar in Fairfield, Iowa as the feature act for a comic I'd worked with a few times earlier in 2007. Relationships are important on the road, and it's always good to know the person you're working with, and even better to get along with them. There are so many variables with being a touring comic, so many random possibilities, things that can go wrong, knowing what you're dealing with as far as the other comic goes takes a huge burden off your mind.

It was a mid-week show, a Wednesday night gig. They had us in a back room of the sports bar, and I was already a little flustered because the battery in my guitar's pickup died during soundcheck and I had to run to a local pharmacy to buy a new one, which made me run a touch late, so folks were already seated before I had the chance to set up and test my gear. I did what I always do: tuned my guitar and played a little bit of "I Remember You" by Skid Row. They reacted well to that, clapped and wanted more. That tends to happen when I soundcheck in front of people. They want me to finish the song or play a different song, or another song, or whatever. If I agree, then they sometimes end up acting slighted when I have to stop, so I grew to just politely decline right away out of experience. I told them I'd be back on in a bit.

About ten minutes and a lackluster introduction later, I got up onstage and did my act. When you're performing and expecting a laugh, you take a slight pause so when the audience laughs it doesn't cover the next line you say, so your next setup or punchline isn't laughed over. It's called holding for applause or holding for a laugh, and I held for a laugh in all the usual spots. Nothing. They were just staring. Not joking, not hyperbole, just… staring.

It's difficult to adequately explain the exchange of energy between a performer and an audience, but I'll try. It's a cycle of sorts, and the more energy an audience gives a performer, in terms of positive reaction, applause, laughter (if its comedy), the more energy the performer has to work with, to put back into the act. It's like using an appliance plugged in to a renewable power source as opposed to having it run on batteries. It sounds like wish-washy metaphysical bullshit, but it's true. Sit enough people close to the stage (because distance kills energy. Really). Sit them close to the stage, where the perfumer can see them react to the show in a positive manner, and the performance changes—charges. The performer gains energy to pour back into the audience, which then almost always returns it once again to the stage. No one gets tired. Everyone remains in this heightened emotional state, feeling more than they were before the show. It's symbiotic.

But here, no one was responding. I got stares from everyone, literal agape, slack-jawed stares in some instances, followed by polite applause after my songs. I was getting nothing back from them, so again I did what I usually do. I poured even MORE energy in, and then even more. I upped the energy, upped the effort, magnified myself even further, determined to project into and through them, to reach some place in them that would let them laugh, make them enjoy the show. Silence. Stares. Polite applause.

I grew frenetic. It was a half hour slot, an act I'd done several times, pretty much word for word, verbatim, filling up thirty-minute slots all year. With the right applause breaks, I'd had to cut material. I finished my act in Fairfield, Iowa in just over twenty-three minutes. During the next to last song, I pitched my merch, but only because I was desperate to fill up time. I was selling the *Past Tense* CD and "It's A Licky-Licky Night" t-shirts. I finished my show well more than five minutes early to polite applause and introduced the closing comic.

I was drained, despondent. I called Jody from the parking lot, feeling like I'd just bombed. I'd given more and more of myself every minute, every line, every song of the act, and felt like I got nothing in return. She was, well, Jody. She knew there were bound to be bad nights and handled me well, told me to take a minute and then go set up for merch and get something to eat. I took a deep breath, looked at the passing cars outside the sports bar, and went back inside.

Even through the door, the other comic seemed to be getting a much better response than I was. I ordered a burger and set up my CDs and t-shirts, wondering why I was even bothering. When the other comic finished, also under his allotted time I might add, there was a huge round of applause and then everyone came pouring out of that back room, making a bee line for me. I had barely enough time to worry if I'd offended them, if they were coming in an angry mob to lynch me, when I was hit by a barrage of compliments and fistfuls of bills and sold a ton of product that night.

I asked the bartender about the audience later, and he said he'd never seen them act like that. I still don't know what was up, what happened, why they behaved that way, but I figured out that if they're staring at you, they're at least paying attention. I had focused on giving the best show I could and continued to up my game throughout, and somehow it paid off.

In the end, though, happy as I was to have sold the merchandise, and as redeemed as the show felt, I was drained, felt like I could sleep for a week. But I got up early the next morning and drove home. I had another show that weekend, on our oldest' s tenth birthday, but at least it was in Muncie, close to home. I wouldn't miss much that time away from him, and the extra money would be a nice financial pad for the weekend.

Yeah, merch money is nice, but you just can't count on it and you shouldn't have to. I'm not a traveling T-shirt salesman anymore. I sell some CDs and flash drives after my shows, and occasionally something else—something small and easily transported and stored. When I'm at conventions I don't even bring t-shirts anymore. It costs to produce and transport them, and you always end up with sizes that you can never move. I still have a few random shirts—smalls and mediums and one 3X I think—taking up room in storage. Wasted money. I put my shirts online, now. The profit is much smaller, and the shirts cost more, but I don't have to make them or ship them or transport them or count them or roll them. I don't have to manage inventory. I don't have to anticipate sales trends. For the most part, I just have to make music. But let's get back to DragonCon in 2015.

One of the perks of performing at DragonCon is that they'll give you a table out with the rest of the musicians. 2016 was the last year I accepted that particular perk, and for a very simple reason: they expect you to have that table manned as much as possible during regular convention hours, and for me? That's a hassle. I've got stuff I want and need to do, so I stopped accepting the offer. I never sold much merch at the table, anyway, though maybe that speaks to my deficiency as a salesperson. One thing I *did* get to do at that table, though, was hang out with my performer friends. Sean Smith has been with me at most of the DragonCons I've attended and performed with me on guitar and singing harmony beginning that year, but at the moment, in 2015, he was off enjoying the convention while I sat and stood and yawned at the table. My table was almost always next to the Blibbering Humdingers' table, and that year found us in the bowels of the of the Marriott, near one of the large Main Programming rooms.

I was bored and though there were many people around us, none were paying much attention to us. They were looking at cosplay, having discussions, and waiting for a volunteer to tell them they could begin lining up for the next panel. There was already a panel going on in that large room—I think it was a Q&A with Stephen Amell from TV's *Arrow* at the time, but the volunteers wouldn't allow anyone to line up for the next panel yet. It just wasn't time.

Here's something you need to know about DragonCon, if you've never been: the lines are long. Ponderously long. They become vast, huge things with lives of their own, and convention staff and volunteers have implemented a set of protocols to help control and herd these unwieldy things. One of those protocols is by using colored tape on the floor to lay out a maze-like area, something to emulate rope stanchions, but much more affordable and easier to replace if damaged or stolen. These taped-off lanes indicate where and in what direction the crowd should queue once they are allowed to begin forming a line. This results in an oddity of human nature that I've only witnessed at DragonCon.

The volunteers stand in the taped-off queuing zone, not allowing folks to stand or sit there when it gets closer to the time to begin lining up, and so people begin forming a preemptive queue outside of the designated area. More than one, in fact. Several rival preemptive lines being to form, each vying for the precious and coveted acknowledgement of the DragonCon volunteer as the official first queue, a designation that the volunteers rarely make or acknowledge. These people begin making and waiting in lines for the express purpose of waiting in another line, and I find that *hilarious*.

Like I said, I was bored and no one was paying attention to us, so I started making up a song about it. As I played, sang, and improvised, Kirsten from the Blibbering Humdingers started harmonizing with me, suggesting rightly that I should be singing "waiting to wait in line" as opposed to "waiting to stand in line." Lo, and behold! People had started paying attention to us, so we did it again. Loudly.

We had no amplification, it was just me, my acoustic guitar, and Kirsten Vaughn singing without the aid of modern amplification technology, and the people who were waiting to wait in line loved it. They laughed, they cheered, they sang along. Someone even came over to buy a CD, I think. And then, as we were singing and they were cheering us, the door to the Main Programming room opened and a volunteer came out, telling us we had to stop singing, that the audience in that room couldn't hear the star with the microphone and the expensive sound system. We stopped. The crowd booed, even louder than they were cheering before. I chuckled, all the while waiting to get thrown out of DragonCon and never asked back.

Sean and I performed "Waiting To Wait In Line" at every show we had that weekend, and every audience loved it each time. It was something every single attendee there could enjoy and identify with and has since become a staple of my DragonCon sets, getting performed at least once over the weekend each time I attend.

LYRICS - OLIVER REED

Fare thee well my old friend,

    If I could toast to every smile you brought, the drinks would never end.

    But still the wake, it falls to me,

    And though I don't know where to turn to, even blinded men could see,

It'll take more than a pint or two to celebrate your life.

    I'll need a bender so legendary

    That mortal men will shudder when they think of the night

    I went drinking like Oliver Reed.

I'll raise a pint. No, make it eight.

    Twelve double rums and then some whiskey--half a bottle, take it straight.

    And it will be fitting tribute

    To the last round of the only thirst endowed to drink to you.

'Cause it'll take more than a pint or two to celebrate your life.

    I'll need a bender so legendary

That mortal men will shudder when they think of the night
I went drinking like Oliver Reed.

Oliver Reed was a legend with a liver made of fire
    And a thirst that was more of a need.
    And his affair with the bottle danced him to his funeral pyre,
    But I'll go drinking like Oliver Reed.

'Cause I'll need more than a pint or two to celebrate your life.
    I'll need a bender so legendary
    That mortal men will shudder when they think of the night
    I went drinking like Oliver Reed.

21

OLIVER REED

O liver Reed is one of those songs that I wrote long before I ever used it on an album, and also one that I spent a long time trying to write before it got written. In fact, at one point, I gave up trying to write it, resigning myself to the thought that it just shouldn't be written. I first encountered Oliver Reed's body of work through an old horror film: *Curse of the Werewolf* via our local late night horror movie host, Sammy Terry. I saw Reed in many things afterward: *Condorman*, *The Three Musketeers*, and *The Adventures of Baron Munchausen*, among many others.

I enjoyed his work and knew who he was but didn't know much about him until I read that he died after a night of heavy drinking while making his final film appearance as the gruff trainer Antonius Proximo in *Gladiator*. In that one evening he imbibed eight pints of beer, twelve double rums, half a bottle of whiskey, and a few shots of cognac in a drinking match against some sailors on shore leave in Malta. His bar tab alone was almost six hundred dollars in 1999, which is around a thousand dollars today. He beat five of the sailors, one at a time, in arm wrestling contests, and then collapsed of a heart attack and died on the way to the hospital.

There were references in the article I read to his notorious life of excess and alcoholism, and years later, sometime around 2012, I got it in my head that I wanted to write a drinking song. I'd already written "Me and Alan Moore's Beard," and the idea struck me to write about drinking with Oliver Reed. I was in love with the idea, thought it would make for a rollicking, laughing tune—me recalling a fictional night out drinking with this notorious alcoholic known for his bigger than life antics. So, I did what I tend to do when wanting to write about a particular subject that I know little about—I started researching him.

I got very sad, very fast. He was a promising young actor who could have been more, maybe even a huge star, but his alcoholism constantly got in the way. I watched video clips of him on talk shows in the seventies, drunk and making untoward jokes, then in the 80s doing more of the same, and ultimately an appearance on David Letterman where it appears he was drunk and unsure whether Dave was mocking him, and he fluctuated back and forth between charming and silly and angry drunk, sometimes seeming as if he was just looking for a target to lash out at. I read about how Ridley Scott, the director of *Gladiator*, made him promise that he wouldn't drink during filming, and that he worked around it by drinking on the weekends, when he wasn't on the call sheet. I learned about how another actor, Omid Djalili, tried to cover for him a little, saying in an interview that Reed "hadn't had a drink for months before filming started..." and that it was "tragic. He was in an Irish bar and was pressured into a drinking competition. He should have just left, but he didn't."

He became human to me. I could see how damaged he was, how flawed, how broken, despite his talent and skill and success, and I didn't want to write the song anymore. I didn't want Oliver Reed to *be* the joke; I wanted him to be the *pathway* to a joke. So I gave up the idea of writing a song about him—or even about a night of irrevocable drunkenness. Like Faulkner said, "in writing you must kill all your darlings," so I put it away, or so I thought. In reality, I just put it aside.

For Christmas of 2013, my mother-in-law gave me a mandolin. She's also why I play a ukulele, now, too. If buying me Christmas presents were a competition, she'd win most years, though I'm sure Jody plays at least a small part in that. I'd never asked for a mandolin, never considered playing one, but it was a fantastic present, and I loved it then and still do.

Then, on January 30, 2014, my friend and co-owner of The Fickle Peach Brion Fickle passed away after a long, brutal fight against cancer. I'm still not sure his business partner and best friend, Chris Piche (another great guy and dear friend of mine), has ever recovered from the loss, or ever fully will. Brion and I weren't close as friends go--many of my friends were much, much closer to him--but I respected him and he was always a supporter of mine and a genuinely great guy. He played mandolin in a small, local band called Pray for Mojo (not the one you can find on Spotify. Although they released a CD, it's not available streaming anywhere to my knowledge). When February came, I had already committed myself to February Album Writing Month, and somewhere between Brion's memorial and learning to play the mandolin a bit, and having the pressure to write songs, everything clicked and the song just fell together. Oliver Reed would no longer be the joke, not even the path to a "joke joke," but more the path to a salute to both Oliver and all friends lost.

I wasn't particularly proficient at the mandolin—I'm still not. This was my first time recording with one, and I'd been playing for just over a month. I wasn't accustomed to writing elegies or dirges and I'm still not. I don't want to get in the habit of it, either. I'm not accustomed to friends dying, for that matter, but it happened more than once in 2014 alone and the older I get, the more people who I love are going to, and have, died. It's simple math, and simple reality, and it sucks on a deep and profound level.

I love the song, and I cannot play it without thinking of Brion, or Tommy who passed in June of 2014, or my mom who passed in May of 2015, or of dozens of good people who passed before and since. It is a bittersweet celebration of life and of our imperfections, Oliver's as a human, mine as a human and as a songwriter, humanity's imperfections in general, and it's one way I continue to feel connected to people I love who passed on.

I hope you never need a song for that reason, but if you do, there it is.

LYRICS - DRUNKARDS AND PHILOSOPHERS

I sit back And let the beer ease through me. I can feel it in my teeth
I'd fall down If I tried to reach the bedroom and I'm too damned
drunk to sleep.
And so I get all sentimental like all good drunkards do
And I look back on my life and everything that I've been through
Cause the beer makes the past stronger, it makes the hurt last
longer
And it reaches back through years
And though it makes the present cloudy, the past comes crystal
clear.

Looking back farther, ever, than before.
Cars that I bought and the men that I've fought and the women I
fought them for
They say learning don't come easy, but ignorance ain't free
There are prices in our lives that we pay but we can't see
But the beer works like an x-ray cutting through your memories
Til you even see the bones. But no-one wants to hear about it
So I'll just sit and drink my beer alone.

If I could turn back time, I would drink a lot less now.
    Or at least that's just the way it seems to be.
    It's just some meaning to life that we're all looking for, somehow,
    The drunkards, the philosophers, and me.

And somehow I've lost my balance, but I'll find it again
    Cause a lifetime moves in cycles and I drink a kind of zen
    Until I am the beer inside me, flowing through my veins until I
somehow find myself
    And all the memories that have made me are in there somewhere
locked up on a shelf.

If I could turn back time, I would drink a lot less now.
    Or at least that's just the way it seems to be.
    It's just some meaning to life that we're all looking for, somehow,
    The drunkards, the philosophers, and me.
    The drunkards, the philosophers, the die-hards and the not-so-
sures, the poets, the
    philanthropers, the pure-breads and the mangy curs, the drunk-
ards, the philosophers, and
    me.

22

DRUNKARDS AND PHILOSOPHERS

D runkards and Philosophers" was written sometime in 2002 or 2003. I can tell you the house we lived in when I wrote it, but I don't have a ton of notes or even exact dates. A few years ago, I might have been able to give you an exact date, but I've since undertaken a sizable purge of stuff from my lair/studio, and my best hope for an exact date (or something extremely close) would come from checking the file date on one of dozens of burned CDs or DVDs I surrendered to the trash back then. Although I feel a little frustrated about it, I'm mostly laughing at myself for feeling frustrated because having an exact date on this is not that important. I have to keep reminding myself that giving up the self-imposed role of being some curator of a boxed and stored museum of my own past was the right thing to do, because my instinct is to save it all, to be the pack rat, to reserve a spot on that *Hoarders* TV show.

Anyway, this was around the time that I was making THE DECI-SION™: the big decision of what to do with my life, what goal to pursue. There were a handful of songs written around that time that were serious songs that at some point made it to release in some form: "C'Mon Barbara," "Legends," "Trickle Down," "Cling" (the song that became "Impotent Nerd Rage"), and "Drunkards & Philosophers."

There are other serious songs written or recorded around that time that haven't seen circulation on an official Mikey release: "Fall Away From Yourself" was written in 1992 or '93 but I also recorded a version of it around the time in question. There is a song called "I Remember" that I wrote and recorded around then that may never see the light of day. There was a song called "Guide" that I had started to write then and never finished until February Album Writing Month in 2020, I think. It can be found on my Patreon.

There were other songs that I wrote in that period and never recorded: off the top of my head I can think of "Hold Me Down" and "She Says"— I still have the original drafts or partial drafts of those songs in hardcopy form in the box of old songs, partial songs, line ideas, and scribbles that I occasionally pore back through for inspiration, like some tome of untold wonders—yes... Let's pretend that's what I call it. *The Tome of Untold Wonders.*

Jody and I were karaoke regulars back then and I had just gotten to the point of drinking and being interested in beer. I was either rehearsing with an unnamed cover band on the extreme north side of Indianapolis or with an improv comedy troupe named Tantrum in Indianapolis. I can't remember which it was, though it could have been either, or both. They were consecutive parts of my life, with a small island of concurrence.

I tell a story sometimes about how I have interests and talents or perhaps skills or maybe just inclinations towards certain creative areas in multiple fields, things that I was interested in and maybe talented or skilled in, and how I felt, emotionally and from a sense of purpose and accomplishment, like I was treading water in the middle of a lake. I was facing the metaphorical prospect of drowning and I needed to pick a direction and swim to shore. I talk about this a lot when people want to discuss how I've got to where I'm at right now. I felt pressured, so I narrowed down my options to things that I could do in addition to making a living and, realizing that I wanted to perform and that music was a huge part of it, I asked Jody whether she thought I should pursue serious music or comedy. She thought about it and said I should pursue serious music.

Of course I chose comedy, not because I was being contrary, but because of what happens when you present yourself with two options and you flip a coin. If you don't prefer one outcome to the other, you'll go with whatever that coin flip tells you to do, but you know that if the coin lands on heads and you say, "Well... Best two out of three," that what you wanted was the other option. I knew in the moment between asking Jody and her answer that what I wanted was comedy, that I thought or felt it was the right path, even if it wasn't necessarily what I wanted for my entire life. So that's where I put my time and effort, ultimately.

I left the cover band and went with the comedy troupe, and eventually the funny music, and stopped concentrating on the non-comedic music, like "Drunkards and Philosophers." When I wrote the song, I was spending a lot of time soul-searching, feeling guilty about my newly finalized divorce and how I'd treated everyone in the situation: my son, my ex-wife, Jody, even myself. To say I was being self-centered would be an understatement. I'm better now, I hope, but that was a time of internal crisis for me on many levels, and "Drunkards and Philosophers" is a song that showcases that inner conflict, that introspection, and ultimately a search for meaning, direction, and connection.

There are lyrics in the song I'm proud of having written. "They say learning don't come easy, but ignorance ain't free. There are prices in our lives that we all pay but we can't see." I thought I knew the depth of that line when I wrote it, but every day I'm alive I seem to find some newer, deeper piece to it that I hadn't felt before, either in my own direct experiences or indirectly, observed through the experiences of my friends and loved ones. I've also always been fond of the phrase "I drink a kind of zen," which has its own implications about the effects of alcohol and the act of consuming it.

And then there's the bit that has always reminded me of the end of "Rainbow Connection." "The drunkards, the philosophers, and me" isn't that far removed from "the lovers, the dreamers, and me," but it began with a night where I was drinking beer and realized that I couldn't feel my teeth, and Jody and I had a good laugh about it. She swears she can still remember what I was wearing that night. Me? Not so much. I might have nearly fallen while trying to reach the bedroom.

A version of the song was recorded, just guitar and vocals, and I've probably still got it around somewhere on an old hallowed hard drive (I remove all the hard drives from old computers and keep them, like a good, paranoid hoarder). But then, like all of the serious music I wrote at the time, the song was shelved until I was trying to find geeky material for my second album, and decided to un-retire the song, make it a punky, driving rock song, and change the line "the Drunkards & Philosophers & Me" to "right here in my beer-powered time machine." I'm sure that this decision had nothing to do with the *Barbarian Jetpack* album coming out on November 15, 2012, and my announcement of my new-at-the-time podcast, *Beer Powered Time Machine* on November 14, 2012. None at all.

Sometime in 2013 or 2014, I played the original version of the song at a filk circle, most likely at MarsCon in Williamsburg, Virginia. If you're not familiar with the concept of filk music, a majority of the people who know of filk, but aren't active participants, think of it as parodies of songs where the lyrics have been changed to be about fantasy or science fiction media, usually books. Some folks think of it as the "music of fandom." I think of it as a community where people sit in a circle and take turns listening to and playing along with each other as they sing songs about their respective fandoms. Sometimes these songs are parodies, sometimes originals, but the overall goal is to create a supportive, respectful, and encouraging atmosphere to people of all skill and talent levels as they celebrate their fandoms through music. I'm sure other people have other descriptions or definitions, but—this being my book and all—we'll go with mine for now. Chuck Parker, World's Okayest Bassist and a good friend and musician, preferred it to the *Barbarian Jetpack* version, or even the slowed down, acoustic rendition of the *Barbarian Jetpack* version that I'd taken to performing on occasion. Several folks agreed with him—myself being one of them—and it made me excited to do the song again.

When the *detour* album rolled around and I started thinking about what material to include, since it was a "serious" album, I jumped at the chance to include the original "Drunkards & Philosophers" on it, as well as "Trickle Down," "C'mon Barbara," and "Legends," although "Legends" had already been released on the album *Tentacow*, and "Drunkards & Philosophers" and "Goonies (Never Say Die)" had already appeared in high-energy, rock forms on the *Barbarian Jetpack* album back in 2012.

I love this song, and I number parts of it (and therefore the entirety of it, by default) among the best songs I've ever written. I did have an annoying friend who referred to it as the X-Ray Beer song, but I haven't seen him in a long time, and I wonder if that's a coincidence. I don't know. Each lifetime moves in cycles, and I guess I'll keep drinking a kind of zen. For now, at least.

LYRICS - LEGENDS

Like a faded old parchment, this map of my life lies here before me
tonight.
    All the paths laid out for me, my career and my wife, and the
choices I've made, wrong
        and right.

I need a life that's not written in blood or in stone,
    Wanna tear from this page and stand on my own,
    And when history is written, I'll write mine alone,
    Legends are born in this way.

For uncharted waters, the sailors of old used dragons to mark on
the map.
    I'm drawn to these waters on the map of my life, the only place
where there's no path.

I need a world of blank pages to sail upon
    In the unexplored space 'tween the dusk and the dawn.
    I'll ride on those dragons and see what's beyond.
    Legends are born in this way. Legends are born because

Legends are born in blank spots on the map where the pages are worn thin by
 Dragons, uncertainties, promises made. Legends are born in this way.

I'm not seeking new worlds in this journey I'm on, just trying to find my own way.
 When you walk down the path that another has drawn, you lose what your voice has to
 say,
 And legends are killed in this way. Legends are killed because

Legends are born in the dragon-marked waters where sailors are warned to just
 Turn back, to go around, just stay away. Legends are born in this way.

I could turn back right now. I could stay where I'm safe, but I won't.
 Though I'm damned if I go, I'll regret my whole life if I don't.

Legends are born in the back rooms of Heaven where dreams end up torn and then
 Nobody rushes in to save the day. Legends are born in this way.

23

LEGENDS

In the summer of 2002, I was part of an improvisational comedy troupe named Tantrum in Indianapolis. I lived about 60 miles away in Muncie, Indiana. That comedy troupe, Tantrum, performed several times over that summer in the Little Tiny Theatre (that was the name of it—the Little Tiny Theatre) in a bookstore in Indianapolis called BookMamas. It was an intimate space, and I'd taken to improvising songs at points during the shows—something I still do, and still remember the first time I did it back in the early 90s —but that's a different story.

We also had friends who were singer-songwriters, and sometimes they'd also perform at the Little Tiny Theatre in BookMamas. Once, Tantrum even opened for a couple of them. At the time I was struggling to find myself as a person, as a comedian, as a songwriter, but I knew I wanted to play as a musician at that show in addition to performing in the troupe.

I had separated from my now ex-wife in September of 2001 (even though the divorce wouldn't be finalized until November of 2004. It's another long story that I won't go too far into but knowing at least that much is pertinent to the song). I was pretty torn up about it inside. I want to say I was torn up despite it being my choice to separate, but I think it was *because* it was my choice to separate. In retrospect it was the right thing to do for many, many reasons that I have no need or desire to talk about, but it tore me up. I was conflicted on an epic scale.

I'd left a cover band I'd been rehearsing with to pursue the comedy troupe, but I still wanted to be a standup comedian as well as a singer/songwriter, so my songwriting was also conflicted. I was writing funny songs and serious songs, working and doing comedy, being separated and navigating the waters towards a divorce, trying to spend time with my son and crying about it, and there was so very much more to unpack going on, including my relationship with Jody. It was emotionally tumultuous.

We were living in a huge blue house on Main Street and I wrote "Legends" in the room I was using as a studio—I called it my cave at the time; I hadn't graduated to a secret lair or studio yet. The song was my attempt in the summer of 2002 to craft a musical mission statement of sorts. I thought it sounded like Tommy Shaw from Styx. I needed to express why I was following the path I was choosing (I hadn't altogether committed to anything yet: divorce, marriage, career, comedy, music...ANYTHING) and I was feeling so guilty, so conflicted, and so raw, while the song felt right.

I wrote it using nautical imagery, with no real idea why. I've never been a sailor, none of my family were sailors or in the Navy or anything remotely similar. It's just the way it came out, the metaphor of my life existing somewhere in the unexplored places on a map, spaces that sailors of old would mark with dragons. I needed to give myself permission to go off the script I'd been writing for myself and find the storyline my life was meant to have.

For years, more than a decade, I had performed the song live only the once, at the Little Tiny Theatre in BookMamas. I was coming down with a cold that day. My voice was cracking because the song was too high for my chest-cold-rattled voice and I was nervous, but one older gentleman approached me after we were done. He'd been there for the whole show, the comedy troupe, my mean, funny songs, the other performers, but still came up to me afterwards and told me that song was important, that it needed to be sung. He was adamant.

I was younger, though, and trying to work out what should come next, and the song disappeared into the uncertain storm clouds of my personal life. Years later, once my path wound its way into standup comedy, and then beyond it into performing at conventions, I played the song in a filk circle and then again, on stage, at the closing Round Robin of MarsCon in Williamsburg, Virginia. I was tentative about performing it, and fought back tears on stage at the roar of applause that followed the closing notes. I said on that stage that *this* is why I knew I was where I was meant to be, because they wanted to listen. They didn't need me to be funny, or exciting, or perpetually "on." They just wanted my music to be genuine. They were my extended family. I belonged.

In 2017, our oldest, Ben, surprised us all by going into the Navy after high school, and the song took on whole new meaning for me. It was like I'd written it backwards in time and couldn't see the meanings or reasons until I reached certain points in my life, our lives. He didn't hear it until he was on leave and brought his fiancée to a small convention I was performing at in Indianapolis, InConJunction. He adored the song, and the story behind it, and I felt like we bonded in a way that we never had, achieved a level of understanding that we'd never before achieved. It was a song for me, and a song for him, both trying to find our own way to who we were meant to be.

It's a song for you, too, for anyone who knows in their heart that they weren't meant to walk the path they found themselves on. It's a signal that it's not too late to alter the trajectory of your life. I wrote the song in the summer of 2002, while dealing with the emotional fallout of changing course after years of marriage and the birth of our oldest son. I was not yet thirty years old. My professional comedy career started in December of 2005, at the age of thirty-three—far older than many starting comics. Our youngest was not yet a year old. I thought I'd found my calling, and maybe I had found a calling, but in April of 2011, I released "She Don't Like Firefly" and another calling found me. I was thirty-eight. That was more than a decade ago.

I've been excited and a little (sometimes far more than a little) afraid at every step, every juncture. I've questioned choices I made and choices I was considering, but I never question that I need to forge my own path to find what fulfills me, which is something that I managed, somehow, to capture in a song written around twenty years and almost half a lifetime ago. Sometimes I talk about wanting to write songs of substance. "Legends," in my mind, is the benchmark those songs have to measure against.

LYRICS - GOONIES (NEVER SAY DIE)

It must be Thursday. I never got the hang of Thursdays cause there's
   Just too many Mondays in my life.
   It's been one long left turn for the last 300 miles
   And it seems everything I need is on the right.

And I feel like giving up, but my mind keeps wandering back
   To that night Brand talked his girlfriend down the well...

Cause me and One Eyed Willie have been talking this thing out
   Pondering life's mysteries, what is it all about?
   And when the world teams up against us,
   We just look it in the eye.
   Then rush in headfirst, screaming Hey You Guys!
   Goonies Never Say Die.

I just feel jaded, defeated and frustrated.
   Keep wishing somehow I could change my face.
   I'm like a sheep inside wolf's clothing, I'm so filled with fear and
loathing,
   And I worry that I'll never find my place.

I'm held hostage by these hotels. I could go out but there's no telling
　　What waits for me out there, except I'm sure that it ain't you.

But me and One Eyed Willie have been talking this thing out
　　Pondering life's mysteries, what is it all about?
　　And when the world teams up against us,
　　We just look it in the eye.
　　Then rush in headfirst, screaming Hey You Guys!
　　Goonies Never Say Die.

Our lives take different courses, we get married, get divorces,
　　Our regrets and our remorses hold us down until we die.
　　So just keep moving forward, onward, up excelsior because
　　Persistence is the one resource we have that won't run dry...

And me and One Eyed Willie have been talking this thing out
　　Pondering life's mysteries, what is it all about?
　　And when the world teams up against us,
　　We just look it in the eye.
　　Then rush in headfirst, screaming Hey You Guys!
　　Goonies Never Say Die.

24

GOONIES (NEVER SAY DIE)

Goonies (Never Say Die)" began as a song I intended to title "Texarkana." I started writing it in March of 2008, around my second time performing at the Electric Cowboy in Texarkana, booked by the Comedy Zone. The chorus was very different, something along the lines of "I'm stuck in Texarkana..." Pretty uninspired, but I loved the verses I'd written.

I was fairly new to being on the road for a living, having done the road comic thing for a year or so, and at the time it was like working a second full-time job. The long drives and hotel stays had started to lose their luster a little, had become more routine. The honeymoon was over, but I was still in love with the work.

To put it in perspective, I'd gone from performing four dates in 2005 and twenty-six dates in 2006, to performing sixty-two dates in 2007. In what seemed a blink, it was March of 2008 and I was already on my twenty-sixth performance of the year, still working a full-time day job all the while. Less than a quarter of the way through the year, I was already almost halfway through the equivalent of my full performance schedule of the prior year, completely through the schedule of the year before that. Things were growing faster for me than they do for many comics.

On reflection, this was one of those songs that started to gel the geeky side of me with the professional entertainer side. I mean, the song is about being road weary and having self-doubt, but I start it all off with a *Hitchhiker's Guide to the Galaxy* reference, "It must be Thursday, I never got the hang of Thursdays," followed by an obscure KISS reference, "and there's just too many Mondays in my life." (Before they formed KISS, Gene Simmons and Paul Stanley were in a band called Wicked Lester that had a tune called "Too Many Mondays." You can find recordings of it circulated online).

"And it's been one long left turn for the last 300 miles and it seems everything I need was on the right," was a way of encapsulating the experience of driving for a living. When driving, left-hand turns are often a big enough pain that your GPS will try to route you around them, but the line also hints at the frustrations of learning that everything you were looking for was in the other direction from which you turned. This was before I had a GPS or a smart phone, and I was relying on printed Google Maps directions on a clipboard, calling Jody for directions when there was a big enough construction mess. It led to lots of very tense, escalated conversations. When we finally got a GPS, it took such a huge strain off our relationship that we referred to it as The Marriage Counselor.

Then, in the second verse I sang, "I just feel jaded, defeated and frustrated. Keep wishing maybe somehow I could change my face." I was giving voice to the realization that, here I was, a very liberal guy performing what was intended to be a generalized satire of a certain aspect of society, one that I grew up in, in order to lampoon it and point out the sheer ridiculousness of it, the inherent callousness and hypocrisy, and that turns out to be the very audience I'm connecting with. They got that it was a joke, they just didn't get that the joke was on them. Ironically, it was their laughter and cheers, their praise and acceptance, that started to make me feel successful, like I was getting somewhere with my career, while at the same time I wanted scream at the top of my lungs that they just didn't get it.

"I'm like a sheep inside wolf's clothing, I'm so filled with fear and loathing, and I worry that I'll never find my place." This caricature I was playing was beginning to wear on me, though I kept it up in some form until I stopped performing standup comedy in 2019. I just made... modifications. I let my liberalism, my education, my vocabulary and erudition shine through in places. I tried to let them know that it was a character being played, and that I was peeking out from behind the character, winking at them.

"I'm held hostage by these hotels, I could go out but there's no telling what waits for me out there, except I'm sure it isn't you," is a line born of profound homesickness. I'd abandoned the song because I was focusing on comedy, which was paying bills and was what I'd committed to, so the song got filed away. In 2012, I was looking through papers for inspiration while writing material for the second geek album, "Barbarian Jetpack." I'd been wanting to write a Goonies-themed song, and it struck me that *The Goonies* was about persistence in the face of adversity and, on a very fundamental level, so was this song I'd been writing called "Texarkana." So I started re-writing, weaving in the Goonies theme, which is about, as I said, persistence, but also rushing in headfirst, screaming, "Hey You Guys!" It was an apt metaphor for my comedy career in general. My naiveté, enthusiasm, and persistence were what made that career happen, with a generous helping of spousal support from Jody, and understanding from the boys and my workplace.

I was on the emotional fence about the song's bridge, but I liked it nonetheless. I just thought other folks might think it sounded kind of weird, with odd choices of rhyming words. "Our lives take different courses, we get married, get divorces. Our regrets and our remorses hold us down until we die. So just keep moving forward, onward, up, excelsior, because persistence is the one resource we have that won't run dry." In the end, I didn't care that the word choices weren't anywhere near the traditional pop songwriter standards. It struck the right balance of scansion, rhyme, tone, and theme. The nod to Stan Lee added another dimension of geekiness to the song that I loved, and it hammered home the theme of persistence in the face of adversity.

Years later, in July of 2015, when I performed at Confluence in

Pittsburgh, Rand Bellavia of the incredible Ookla The Mok came up to me after my show to compliment me, very specifically, on that bridge, saying that it showed the kind of creativity in rhyme and sound songwriting structure that a lot of music lacks these days. It remains one of the best compliments I've ever received from a fellow musician and it reminded me that I should trust in my instincts and my craft, to write songs that make me happy, and not always try to write for an audience.

I think it works, because people have tended to react well to my music since I've been doing just that. Sometime earlier that year, I was sitting on a stool in the kitchen at home, playing guitar, and I played the song with a slow and melancholy feel, for some reason. Jody told me that I should never play it the other way ever again. I listened to her, and I've rarely played it at the original speed since. When I recorded my first "serious" album, *detour*, I put that slowed, pared down version of "Goonies (Never Say Die)" on it.

I find it odd how many people identify with the song. When I was writing it, I loved it, but I just never saw it in my head as a big crowd pleaser. Somehow, though, people like it (and very much more so as a slower, acoustic song). I won't complain.

25

WAHOOCON

A few years ago, I was at a smaller convention. It my second appearance there and I enjoyed and supported it, but I'm not going to mention the name because the story involves somebody who was either volunteering or working there, I'm not sure which. I'm not here to call anybody out or embarrass anyone, but I did think it was a funny story, so I'm going to tell it.

I was having dinner the night before the convention began, joined by the chairpersons and some of the staff. We were having a great conversation and one staff brought up that she'd met me before when I performed at another convention, one that I'll refer to as WahooCon (though that was not the name, but we have to call it something and it's not my intention to embarrass anybody).

I said, "Really? I don't think I've ever... No, I've never been to that convention."

"No, no, no. You were, you were one of the guests," she said. "I was on the programming committee."

I began the all-too-familiar process of second-guessing myself. I *have* performed at quite a few conventions, and she was talking about one nearly a decade before, at least seven or eight years prior, so I rolled with her assertion that I had played there. She said that they had a great time, everybody loved me, and she was super glad to be working with me again. Apparently, I was very professional and very entertaining at this event I had no recollection of appearing at. Nothing ill was being said of me, so I went with it because a win's a win.

I've been known to have a few drinks at conventions. and have even not remembered that I had already met someone at a previous performance that I'd been stone sober for, but she was talking about a time when I was really focused on getting into and performing at conventions. I had a distinct memory of applying to WahooCon, and just as distinct a memory of not being booked by them. Still, I didn't say anything to that effect. There was no point in pushing the issue. If I'd done so, the most plausible outcomes would have been either to embarrass her or, more likely, make me look like a jerk. Worst case scenario: both. I was more interested in being involved than being right, in making sure everybody had a good time.

That's what I see my real job as, you see. Whenever I'm appearing at an event, I see it as my responsibility to try and make sure everybody there has the best time possible, including the staff and the volunteers. If somebody is going to have a miserable time at a convention I'm working, I would rather that person be me. That way everybody else has a great time and walks away with a fantastic memory that I'm involved with, even if it's just on a peripheral level.

Later that night, in my hotel room, while talking with Jody on the phone, I told her of the dinner conversation and she said, "Yeah, I don't think you've ever been to WahooCon."

I said, "I don't think I have either," and started looking through my emails. Trivia time: I save emails. I'm kind of an email hoarder. So, I was scrolling page after page, message after message, until I found what I was looking for. I read Jody the email from the programmer at WahooCon, the very person from dinner who was insisting that I'd played WahooCon, except in the polite and brief email, I was informed that they wouldn't be able to use me or find a place for me to perform at WahooCon that year. Earlier in the evening, I'd been told that I was listed on the WahooCon website as having been there, so I went and checked the convention's website. It turns out that, on that year, they had a list of attending guests. My name was included among them.

I was baffled, because I was never there. In fact, I had the rejection email from the very person who was insisting that I'd been there. It's a strange feeling, having been to a convention that I was never at. At least non-existent me made a great impression on somebody. It appears that a decade or so before, a doppelgänger Mikey walked a convention hall somewhere in the middle of the South, and did a great job. Maybe he even sold some CDs, I don't know. All I know is that more than once over the course of the weekend, this person was emphatic and mentioned to multiple people that we had worked together, that she had booked me at this other convention.

I just smiled and went along because I felt as if correcting her would end in a negative manner, even if I was right. As long as she was happy to have worked with me, and as long as fictional me didn't do something horrible, I'm fine. I'm sure that fictional me also did an incredible job of trying to make sure everybody had a good time because I'm still listed on their website as having been a guest at a convention that I never attended, that I've still never been to, years and years later.

There are times when being right, when winning the argument, just isn't worth it, where being right is perhaps the socially wrong thing to do, maybe even the moral or ethically wrong thing to do. Maybe we should all try and work on doing right as opposed to being right, though I too often still get hung up on the idea being right. Sometimes you just have to let go of things, at least publicly, at least until you have a book deal and decide to tell the story. Just don't give any names, alright? Just don't give any names.

See you at WahooCon.

LYRICS - A HUFFLEPUFF
(KNOCKED MY HOUSE ELF UP)

I have a cottage in a wizarding village and lately my life's pretty rough

Because the family next door moved out and my new neighbor's a Hufflepuff.

Now Hufflepuffs are damn fine wizards, Tri-Wizard Tournament Runners-up.

And you may never find a friend more loyal, or more deserving of Helga's cup, but

This Hufflepuff knocked my house elf up. A Hufflepuff knocked my house elf up.

And now she just makes sandwiches and won't do other stuff...

A Hufflepuff knocked my house elf up.

I used to host some lovely parties, one was attended by Dumbledore.

But ever since my house elf's pregnant she doesn't help with them anymore.

To make it worse, it's not like he loves her. This badger loves to drop his shorts.

Something he had done in the owl room got him kicked out of Hogwarts

This Hufflepuff knocked my house elf up. A Hufflepuff knocked my
house elf up.
 And now she just makes sandwiches and won't do other stuff...
 A Hufflepuff knocked my house elf up.

It's not exactly glamorous
 A Hufflepuff so amorous,
 A deviant whose doinking every
 Creature he can find.
 He had a go at Hagrid's dog.
 He even nailed a chocolate frog
 A bowtruckle, a bludger,
 and a golden snitch three times.
 The monster book of monsters, too,
 And Crookshanks in the common room
 A leprechaun, a grindylow,
 the garden gnomes outside.
 He buggered a blast ended skrewt.
 He diddles to that book by Newt.
 The Gringotts goblins filed a suit
 and won't let him inside, cause

This Hufflepuff knocked my house elf up. A Hufflepuff knocked my
house elf up.
 And now she just makes sandwiches and won't do other stuff...
 A Hufflepuff knocked my house elf up.

REQUIEM FOR A HUFFLEPUFF

In September of 2016, I was back at DragonCon, hanging out at my table in the Marriott, joking around with the Blibbering Humdingers: Scott and Kirsten Vaughn and Chuck Parker (World's Okayest Bassist) about how I was going to request to not have a table anymore. During one of those long periods of not selling anything to the myriad disinterested convention-goers, I made up a song while I was playing guitar with Chuck: "A Hufflepuff Knocked My House Elf Up." It's a habit, a thing I do, maybe even a party trick. I enjoy improvising songs. Kirsten often laments that Scott is very meticulous and planned about writing songs, whereas I just tend to spout off and make them up on the spot. We're different creators with different methods, though, and there's just not much to be done about it.

To truly understand the origin of the song, you need to know that The Blibbering Humdingers have a song called "No Shame in Hufflepuff," in which they joke that "Hufflepuffs are good at making sandwiches, and breathing, and lots of other stuff." I riffed on that in my song, complaining that my pregnant house-elf "just makes sandwiches and won't do other stuff." We were laughing and joking,

Chuck and I playing, and Scott just looked at me and mouthed "I hate you." It was a moment.

I performed the song live for the first time that weekend. It was a rough, unpolished version, nowhere near as polished as the previous year's "Waiting To Wait In Line," but the audience enjoyed it. I continued to develop the song, thinking it would make a good addition to the next full-length geek rock comedy album I put out. I'd already released *Tentacow* and then *detour* in 2016, and 2017 only saw the release of the Bitey Little Blighters EP *Bitten*, so the next full-length album I produced was *Driven*, released in March of 2018, and I was determined to put "Hufflepuff "on it.

The original recording had a different vibe, and truly seemed to be ripping off "Father Christmas" by the Kinks. It was making me miserable, and I considered scrapping the tune until I received tracks from Trent Wilson (from Big Damn Heroes and Transylvania out of Springfield, Missouri). His guitar work was amazing and the tracks he provided transformed the song, helping me hear it through new ears and in a new light. I told him after the album came out that I kind of wished I could redo the song lyrics, because his guitar work had energized it, made it into something more than I had imagined.

He said, "It's your song. You can do what you want with it."

He was right, of course, but I left it. Almost a year later, at MarsCon in January 2019, I learned that at least one member of a music group there judged me in quite a negative light because of the song, because they thought that since a house-elf is required to consent to requests and demands, there isn't any actual consent, so the overtone of a house-elf getting impregnated implied rape. Part of me internally railed against this idea. It wasn't what I intended at all. In my head (and hell, it feels silly even saying this out loud, but...) it was a consensual relationship between the house elf and this sexually promiscuous Hufflepuff.

I know it might seem ridiculous to some, but I can follow their logic on this and it bothered me. It BOTHERS me. I am not what many would call a social justice warrior, but I *am* a person who wants to truly be supportive of my fellow people—all of them, all genders, all sexual orientations, all belief systems—and it's something that is important to me. I accepted long ago that I can't control how people interpret my art, my music, and sometimes that means that they see something there that I didn't intend and sometimes that I don't see, myself, but when something like this is pointed out to me and I end up seeing anything in it that causes me to feel the need to defend my own work to myself—then I also have to acknowledge that perhaps it's not worth defending.

I stopped performing "A Hufflepuff Knocked My House Elf Up" in late 2019. Part of me was sad because I loved the fast, verbose bridge —"It's not exactly glamorous, a Hufflepuff so amorous, a deviant who's doinking every creature he can find..." Being able to fit that many syllables into that short of a span is an accomplishment, it's impressive, and there are very few audiences who seemed to appreciate the Herculean task that it was, both to write and to perform.

I enjoyed the creation of the song, loved its musical execution and evolution. It's one of those songs where I feel the need to rework the lyrics if it's going to have a future. Either that, or I'll have to find a way to get past the problematic nature of the fictional, hypothetical sexual relationship between the Hufflepuff and... well... anyone. And the problem, in my eyes, *does* lie entirely with the Hufflepuff, because the house elf in the song has shown they can refuse to do anything but make sandwiches when she chooses, which means she absolutely and unequivocally has free will. The same can't be said for the litany of other creatures the Hufflepuff accosted, and I'd prefer not to make non-consensual sex a joke, because it isn't.

On the other hand, I am on record as having wanted the song to be better than it was in the first place, wanting the lyrics to be better than they were, and here is my excuse to do just that—if I choose to take the opportunity. I don't know. I don't see myself doing so anytime soon, but it might happen. Trent was right—it's my song. I can do whatever I want with it: perform it, let it sit, or rewrite it.

On a side note, in February of 2019, Sean Smith and I performed for the first time as the Varlots at the Kentucky Pirate Festival. We'd been booked by friends of mine, Bob and Dieter from Drunk & Sailor, an established pirate act. We wore costumes and eyeliner, and did material crafted for the act, a pirate act aimed at Renaissance Faires and festivals and the like. The Varlots were invited by Drunk & Sailor to play a couple of songs at the big main stage show at the end of the festival. We played a song called "Nothing But Pirates" to general amusement, but then Dieter (the Drunk from Drunk and Sailor) asked me to perform Hufflepuff. I agreed, he introduced the song, and it went over very well. After I left the stage, as I wandered to the bathroom, someone stopped me outside the bathroom and recognized me.

"You're Mikey Mason," he said, and I acknowledged it as the truth.

"I was angry for a minute there, you can ask my friends," he said. "I didn't recognize you and I was fuming about that guy passing off a Mikey Mason song as his own!" We laughed, and I thanked him, and then drove home late in the evening with Sean in pirate boots and eyeliner. You know, a typical Saturday night.

LYRICS - THE OPPOSITE OF COOL

I care a little too much, I laugh a little too loud.
   I look a touch out of place but still blend in with the crowd,
   And I was always picked last for everything at my school.
   I am the opposite of cool.

And I still read comic books, I've got a long box or nine.
   Got a house full of cats, I post their pictures online.
   I wear the shirt of the band whose concert I'm going to.
   I am the opposite of cool

I get a little too mad, I cry a little too much.
   I return every text but I still feel out of touch.
   I get excited for things and want to share them with you.
   I am the opposite of cool.

I love some movies you don't and don't like some that you do.
   I'm more a red-shirt than Kirk and I still watch Doctor Who
   And I know which Hogwarts house that I'd want sorted into.
   I am the opposite of cool.

MIKEY MASON

I've got my head in the cloud, I've got my feet on the ground,
    I've got my nose to the grindstone but there's no one around.
    I've got my head screwed on tight, got my priorities straight,
    And every breath is a fight but I'm feeling great

I don't have too many friends and I still answer my phone.
    I just don't know how to dance unless I'm drunk or alone.
    I shouldn't care what you think but I still probably do.
    I am the opposite of cool.

27

THE OPPOSITE OF COOL

Sometimes songs take a long time to write. Sometimes they sprout from your mind like Athena from Zeus' forehead, fully formed and leaving you wondering how that got in there. Most often, it happens somewhere in-between.

A night or two before I wrote "The Opposite of Cool," I made a huge ass out of myself in public. I was at the Fickle Peach with friends playing Euchre. I wasn't drunk by any stretch—I'd had three beers over a four-hour period. There was some ribbing going on, and I can't remember the details of what was happening, but I got inordinately angry. I'd been experiencing emotional issues at the time, anyway, intense feelings of anger or sadness. Sometimes I would bust out crying or get misty watching a commercial. Other times minor annoyances would turn me into a raving, rambling, angry mess. That night I just erupted, screaming, incapable of having a reasonable conversation, and at first my friends were laughing. They thought I was doing some bit or something, and that triggered me further, and rather than let it get worse, I did the only thing I felt I could that would allow me control over the situation. I left. I walked out into the cold, January night and called Jody after a bit, as I was walking home. She insisted on driving out to pick me up. It was uncharacteristic of me, a clear signal that something was wrong, and it was embarrassing to me on a personal level. Of course, later I apologized to my friends and have yet to accept the offer to play a game of Euchre since.

A day or two later, I had apologized to my friends and I was working on material for the new album and the first line that came out was, "I get a little too mad, I cry a little too much," and it just felt true in a way that many lines don't or can't. I've found that I cry more readily the older I get. I'm not sure why, and it's been an adjustment, but I've become okay with it. Things like that are easier to deal with, if you know they're likely to happen. I knew, as the words began pouring out of me, as this song began pouring out of me, that it was going to make me cry, and boy, did it. I was able to record a simple demo of it, just guitar and vocals, but having to do multiple vocal takes because I just kept crying.

It took me three full days to be able to perform the song all the way through without crying. It was as if I'd been writing down who I was as a person, one line at a time, without thinking about it, and it affected me on a raw, emotional level. I know it's popular today to condemn toxic masculinity and to encourage men to experience and express their emotions, something I agree with and have for a long time. Still, this felt like an excessive amount of crying.

After the demo was recorded, I posted it on my Patreon, and also shared it with my youngest, Jack, something I often don't do, as he's typically not that interested in Dad's music so much, anymore. That's to be expected with kids, but this song? I wanted to share it with him. We'd moved the summer before and were living in Muncie for the first time in thirteen years, but Jack wanted to remain in his old school system for at least the next year, and we, as parents, agreed. This meant that I drove him a half an hour to school every day, and picked him up as well. We had an hour of car time to talk and bond every school day, and I had an hour of alone time in the car every school day. He was a seventh grader at the time, and as we pulled out of the school parking lot that day, I asked if he wanted to hear my new song.

"Sure," he said.

I played it through the car's stereo for him, and something interesting happened. Jack was, as I said, a seventh grader at the time, and tended to have his face in a screen at every available opportunity. Somewhere during the first verse, he closed his phone and just sat there, listening to the song. He stayed silent through the whole thing, listening attentively, and when it was done, he asked, "How do you know so much about me?"

It was all I could do not to cry as I was driving home.

I tell that story at shows, sometimes, because it is true and impactful. A lot of people tell me that "The Opposite of Cool" encapsulates who they are as a person, as well. I had ended up writing my personal theme song. I had no idea at the time that I was doing it, but once I'd finished, and once I tried to play it that first time and ended up collapsing in tears, literal huge, racking sobs, I knew that it was a powerful song that needed to be on the album. And while it seems like it was written overnight, that's not quite the case.

The bulk of "The Opposite of Cool" was written in early 2018, but the last bridge in the song, the one right after the guitar solo, is much older. The part that goes, "I've got my head in the clouds, I've got my feet on the ground, I've got my nose to the grindstone but there's no one around, I've got my head screwed on tight, got my priorities straight, and every breath is a fight but I'm feeling great," was written in 1993. It was the chorus to a song I'd written the words for in a band called Signs of Rain. That song, "Tomorrow's Yesterday," was trite and just... bad. I don't have a copy of it, and probably not even a copy of the words, though I remember how it started (and it was not good). I remembered the words to the chorus because they were the only interesting part of the lyrics, followed by the trite and borderline insipid, "Welcome to tomorrow's yesterday."

When a college kid tries to be profound on purpose, it usually doesn't land as intended.

But the rest of the words to the chorus stayed with me, and although they were written for different sounding songs from different genres, they had the same scansion, meter, and rhyme scheme as the bridges I was writing for "The Opposite of Cool." At first, I put them in as placeholder lyrics because they popped out of my mouth and they scanned, but when I looked at them from an overall standpoint, I felt they belonged in the song. The message of, "despite all these seemingly positive things that I'm telling you about myself, I actually feel like a complete outsider. I'm weird and like weird, uncool stuff. I might have it together as well as anyone else and I'm not misdirected or maladjusted, just different, and though it might be hard at times to be different, it feels good to acknowledge myself for who I am as opposed to who or how anyone else wants me to be. Every breath is a fight, but I'm feeling great."

So yeah, sometimes songs take a long time to write. That's probably my longest write time. It took from 1993 to 2018. Twenty-five years. A quarter century. I'm glad I stopped dragging my feet when it comes to songs.

LYRICS - SHINY MATH ROCKS

Be they metal or of stone, or of plastic, you must own them
    Shiny math rocks make the click-clack sound!

See them lined up at the convention
    Little dice goblins, a line too long to mention
    Eyes are twitching, and fingers itching
    Every time they hear that click clack sound

Shiny Math Rocks! Clicky- Clacky!
    Random numbers makey happy
    Shiny Math Rocks! Clicky- Clacky!
    Shiny math rocks make the click-clack sound!

Grubby fingers clutching madly
    As they hear the shiny math rocks clicky-clacky
    Goblins shouting, "Take My Money!"
    Every time they hear that click clack sound

Shiny Math Rocks! Clicky- Clacky!
    Random numbers makey happy

Shiny Math Rocks! Clicky- Clacky!
Shiny math rocks make the click-clack sound!
For your gaming or whatever or your own Geeky Endeavors...
Shiny math rocks make the click-clack sound!
Shiny Math Rocks! Clicky- Clacky!
Random numbers makey happy
Shiny Math Rocks! Clicky- Clacky!
Shiny math rocks make the click-clack sound!

28

SHINY MATH ROCKS

S ometimes writing a song is work, even if it's written in a short time, and sometimes it can take years between writing sessions to give things time to ruminate. But sometimes a song jumps at you. Tristan (who sells dice and pins and jewelry online and at conventions with his wife Shawna, through their business, Geeky Endeavors), posted on Facebook on June 3, 2019:

"I sell shiny math rocks to all the little dice goblins at conventions. When they say, "I don't need more dice," what they are actually telling me is, "I'm going to buy some. Please show me the good stuff."

Yes, I even call them shiny math rocks to my customers. I'll sometimes elaborate with, "They make the click-clack sound," and nod sagely. You really don't want to know how well this works on ya'll as a sales tactic. I'm not entirely proud."

I don't know if his post was the eventual source of the meme, or if he was parroting the meme after seeing it on social media. I never asked him, and I don't think it matters. I can say without a doubt that I never saw a shiny math rocks meme, let alone one that said these things in this way, until after I read his post—but that's proof of nothing. However, upon reading it, I started writing the song in my head.

First, I commented online, "I have this...urge...to...buy something... Clicky-clacky math rocks?"

And then, less than an hour later, I sent Tristan and Shawna a private message that read, "I may have accidentally written and recorded a song about Shiny Math Rocks. It may accidentally contain the words Geeky Endeavors. Purely by accident."

It was a silly song, different from many other songs I'd written, sort of a crossbreed between "Kobolds Ate My Baby" and "Pumpkin Spicemas" with verses sung by Yakko Warner. I wasn't sure how I felt about it, wasn't sure about how I felt about it being on an album, but I knew it was a song that would resonate with gamers, from those who just bought their first set of dice all the way to guys like my friend Moose, who at last count had a collection of well over thirteen *thousand* dice (he's a completist who loves out of print sets). Since Geeky Endeavors sold pins, Shawna suggested I design a Shiny Math Rocks enamel pin, so I did, which is also where the shirt design came from. That was completed on the same day as the song was released.

And when I released the album *M* that July, I knew that I wanted it included as a track for multiple reasons: it was fun, for one. And it was gaming-centric. And I had new merchandise to tie it in with. It made too much sense from a marketing standpoint to include it on the album, so I did, which is also why "Shiny Math Rocks" got played a lot in live performances that summer. It was definitely a decision driven, at least in part, by business, but it was also a lot of fun.

Not long after the song was released, I started seeing the memes online, and people started sending them to me. Again, I don't know if Tristan's post and/or then my subsequent song was the eventual source of the meme, or not, and I don't think it matters. If I could pick the version of history I wanted, I'd of course, say it was Tristan's post combined with my song, but I truly doubt it.

Thus concludes the secret origin of the "Shiny Math Rocks" song. Years later, while playing a private online birthday show, this was one of the songs requested. When one of the watchers commented that the lyrics aligned pretty well with Nirvana's "Smells Like Teen Spirit," I ended up doing an improvised version of that very thing, a verse and a chorus, during the show before letting it fall apart in a gale of breathless laughter. The next week, I rearranged the lyrics of my song to make a parody of Nirvana's and posted it on Patreon. It's not the kind of thing that will ever make an album, but you might have already seen me do it in concert.

Songs like this are like a gift from the universe, and they're exactly why it's important to interact with people and have experiences. Those experiences become fodder for your art, which you then share with people and interact more, having more experiences and perpetuating the cycle. Some of these gifts are fodder for art, others are fodder for stories. Both come from experiences, though.

As a convention performer, sometimes I'm given other gifts, physical gifts. Sometimes it's baked goods. I've been gifted incredible pies and brownies and cheesecakes. Sometimes it's craft beer or good liquor. Sometimes it's cheap liquor that I happen to adore. I've been gifted bottles of low-dollar scotch and high-dollar whiskeys and bourbons and homemade moonshine at conventions, as well as being bought rum-buckets, cocktails, beers, and receiving many sips from flasks. So many fabulous people like to share their favorite beverages with me. I've been given hand-crafted, genetically engineered, stuffed animal monkeys (yes plural), original artwork and prints, CDs and clothing, posters and toys, and even a crocheted version of myself. If I tried to recount ALL of the amazing gifts I've been given since I started performing at conventions, I'd fail, and end up insulting someone by omission.

Getting gifts as a standup comic was a lot rarer for me, though it did happen. For the most part, I've been bought a lot of drinks. At a gig in Charleston, West Virginia, once, I was given a demonstration packet of warming lubricant from a sex toy salesperson, but that's wasn't the weirdest thing I've ever been given. In January of 2013, I was scheduled to do some dates in Iowa at Jokers Comedy Clubs, January fourth in Des Moines and the fifth in Cedar Falls. It was a bit of a drive, around nine hours, and I had friends in Iowa who were coming to hang out with me when I was in Cedar Falls to play board games and have lunch and dinner. I loved it when that was able to happen, and that was a gift of yet another sort, the gift of time.

On January 4, I made that nine-hour drive and checked into my hotel in downtown DesMoines. I had a pretty good show at Jokers—I don't remember anything specific about that performance, other than it went well. I sold merchandise afterwards, and I remember it selling though I don't remember how much, if it was an exorbitant amount or anything. Then this couple came up to me, a man and woman. She introduced herself, told me she loved the show and that she wanted to give me something: her demo reel. And I paused a second and then said okay, because what do you say in that situation? And she handed me a self-labeled, burned DVD in a slim case with a home-printed insert card. The disc had her name —which I don't remember—and the title, "My Night With Ron Jeremy."

She recounted the story of meeting him when he visited a strip club there in Des Moines, how she and her friend (both were dancers at the club at the time, I believe, though I could be remembering incorrectly—it was many years ago) partied with Ron. Illicit substances were very possibly consumed, and then they all three agreed to have adult relations and have the ladies' boyfriends record it with a couple of video cameras. She took that footage and edited it together and made her "demo reel" for adult films, which she then gave me a copy of.

Now, before I go any further, I want to point out without equivo-cation that sex work is real work and deserves respect. Adult films, exotic dances, etc... are a valid and meaningful form of artistic or sexual expression, or both, and I am not about to ridicule or judge anyone who works in the sex industry merely because they are sex workers. Period.

What I did find funny was that it seemed this woman was perhaps looking to find a break into the adult film industry by handing this disc to a road comic at a comedy club in Des Moines, Iowa, which seemed the equivalent of trying to break into the recording industry by giving your grunge band's demo tape to a rodeo clown. It just doesn't make sense. Sure, that rodeo clown *might* have a contact at a record label somehow, and it's conceivable that they even have the sway to get that contact to listen to the demo, but it's still the sort of improbable long shot that it's not worth considering.

I guess maybe, and this is all just speculation, there was some sort of mental association that because comics are in the entertainment business, we might know someone in the adult film industry, which has a certain degree of possible truth to it. We might know someone. You never know who your friends, associates, or acquaintances are connected to, either by work relationship, friendship, or even kinship. But also, why didn't she just post it online? Break into adult entertainment that way? PornHub had been around for years by that time. I just didn't understand.

And so it was that, in the wee hours of the morning, at 12:48 a.m. Eastern time, I tweeted the following: "Happy audience member gave me a copy of her adult film demo reel on DVD after the show. Awesome & strange. Mostly awesome." At the time, I was using an app that let me cross post the tweet to Facebook, which I did (though I have since removed that FB post, for some reason...)

But before I did, a fellow road comic responded: "Oh! You were at Jokers! Welcome to the club!" That's right! This story and gift were made even more strange by knowing that I wasn't the first person—let alone the first road comic—she'd given such a DVD. And now I'm going to answer the inevitable question: did you watch it? The answer is, yes. I looked at it out of curiosity. Poor lighting, no direction, and amateur cinematography combined with drug-fueled and drunken, sub-par and unconvincing performances meant that I didn't watch much of it.

If I had to sum up how I felt about it, I'd be forced to quote a friend who once told me, "The best thing about watching porn is that you don't have to smell it." I'm not sure what that hotel room smelled like, and I'm glad of it. I brought the disc home to show Jody, and I don't think she ever watched any of it. I believe she just took my word for it, but again, I could be wrong. I kept it as a weird souvenir until 2017, when we were moving from Redkey to Muncie, and the change in households required that I downsize my hoard of stuff. (We all did. Moving is no joke.)

I asked Jody if she thought I should keep it, and in typical Jody fashion, she responded something along the lines of, "Well... if you want to, yeah." She understood the bizarre nature of this type of a gift, my fascination and fixation on why someone would just give these away to random people. Was she trying to break into porn by casting some sort of a wide net, some bizarre, extremely wide, net? Was I the late 2013 rodeo clown scratching my head after being handed someone's early 90's grunge band's demo on cassette?

In the end, I tossed it. It's not that the gift wasn't appreciated, but rather that the real gift, the true bringer of joy in this instance, was the story itself. And for that, even if I'm confused as to the motivations behind it, I'll be forever grateful. Also, if you have a 100% legal adult film demo reel that you want to share with me, you know where to find me.

LYRICS - LOOT THE ROOM

I like fantasy and horror, you like 50 shades of gray
    Our love-life stalled so tonight we're gonna role play
    You won't need a police badge or nurse uniform at all
    Tonight our bedroom is a dungeon crawl!

I'll check each and every surface for traps and secret doors, I'm gonna loot the room!
    I'll climb up on the furniture, I'll get down on all fours, I'm gonna loot the room!
    Until every single opening is thoroughly explored, I'm gonna loot the room!
    I'm a gamer, baby, you won't leave here bored… I'm gonna loot the room!

Put on these wings and leather thong and latex rubber horns
    I lit some candles, drew a magic circle on the floor
    And you can be the succubus I tried to summon forth
    We can wrestle for your treasure and then both go back for more

And check each and every surface for traps and secret doors, I'm gonna loot the room!

I'll climb up on the furniture, I'll get down on all fours, I'm gonna loot the room!

Until every single opening is thoroughly explored, I'm gonna loot the room!

I'm a gamer, baby, you won't leave here bored... I'm gonna loot the room!

And I ordered beer and pizza, we can share a hero's feast,
But that'll have to wait until we slay this sexy beast!

And check each and every surface for traps and secret doors, I'm gonna loot the room!

I'll climb up on the furniture, I'll get down on all fours, I'm gonna loot the room!

Until every single opening is thoroughly explored, I'm gonna loot the room!

I'm a gamer, baby, you won't leave here bored... I'm gonna loot the room!

29

LOOT THE ROOM

Years ago, I had an idea for a song while playing *Skyrim* on my woefully outdated PS2 and searching some ruin or another, scrolling the reticle around the screen looking for anything clickable, which either meant I'd find loot or a secret door or whatever. I found myself thinking, "This could be a metaphor for thorough, intense foreplay (and during and after play for that matter)."

It was the afternoon of Thursday, September 4, 2014. I know because I posted this on Twitter and Facebook: "That moment when you're playing Skyrim and start writing an intensely suggestive, geeky song in your head... #GeekRock"

That was the kernel that would, years later, become "Loot The Room" from the *M* album in 2019. It just took a while to get there. Sometimes ideas need expressed right away, other times they need to gestate in your head for a while. Sometimes you might have been inspired to write that song or story or whatever right away, but instead you tell someone the idea, or you post about it on social media, even if only in a vague way, and thus lessen the impetus to write the song or story, as you've already communicated what you had to say in some form. It happens. It doesn't stop the idea from being good—or bad, either, for that matter—but what it *might* do is keep you from acting on that creative impulse right away.

And that is one reason why writers, artists, and other creatives sometimes don't want to talk about their upcoming project, or the one they're working on right now. The mere act of communicating what you're doing can, in some cases, quell the urge to create the thing. Of course, sometimes they can discuss what they're working on or an idea they have in the right company (which is always subjective) and leave the conversation inspired and compelled to create more, better, and faster. There aren't hard and fast rules about inspiration.

But writing? There's one rule: You have to write. You can edit and revise and rearrange later, but only after you've actually written something, so I did write a version of "Loot The Room." Eventually. On Saturday, April 2, 2016, while sifting through the *Tome of Untold Wonders*, I found that scrap, that thread, that nugget, and finally sat down to put the perspiration to the inspiration. I wrote a draft of "Loot The Room," a very ballad-like draft with a chord structure was far, far too similar to another song of mine, "Settle," for my tastes. Still, I'd written the draft and I did a Facebook livestream of the new song I was working on, because Facebook livestreams were sort of a new toy and I was having fun being productive.

I didn't really like the song, though. The words were fine—pretty close to what I wanted, but the music just wasn't there. So, I put the scrawled lyrics sheets away in the *Tome of Untold Wonders* and let it gestate again. After all, I'd put the work in once already, and gave away the joke twice already, once in 2014 and once in 2016, and coming from a background of comedy, as I've talked about before, you don't want to telegraph your punches too much or too often, and the impetus to do the work again was gone, besides. I moved on to other things and let myself be done with it for a while.

More years later, in July of 2019, somewhere amidst the song-writing sessions for the *M* album, I went back to it again. I was playing with chord structures and how I write songs. My usual pattern is to allow either 4 or 8 beats, one or two measures, per chord, unless I'm walking to another chord somehow. I was toying with the idea of cutting that up, having some chords only be two beats long in a verse while others are four, and then having some one-beat transition chords, and I was literally just picking chords in the same scale and trying them out with different timing and spacing, and it grew into this late 70's/early-mid 80's sort of R&B feel.

I liked it, but wasn't sure what kind of lyrics I wanted for it. I went delving back into the *Tome of Untold Wonders*, and one of the first things that found its way to my hand were the hand-written, scrawled lyric sheets to "Loot the Room," and it fit. It took some tweaking and I had to get into a place where I wasn't thinking about it directly, and ultimately, I did the songwriting in three parts: the lyrics (two years or so after the initial idea), the chord structure (another two years on), and then the editing and arrangement of both a couple days later. It was a long, convoluted process for a video game RPG sex joke, but I like the final result. There are so few sexy dance songs about video games, and I'm glad to have entered the pantheon.

As a side note, I sent the track to Sean Faust for keyboards, and he wanted to know what sort of sound I wanted. I tried to explain to him late 70's R&B, but I had to settle for giving him an example of what I heard in my head, so I told him to listen to "You Matter to Me" from Peter Criss's 1978 KISS solo album. He knocked it out of the park. If you're interested in knowing, sonically, where that keyboard/synth sound and style came from, and how it ended up in on one of my albums, I'd suggest you check that song out.

LYRICS - LET'S FAKE SOME MEMORIES

Another day of selling all my time,
    Of showing up for someone else's problems.
    Another day where I can't speak my mind,
    Of wondering if this is hitting bottom?
    The minutes and the seconds creeping by,
    Shackled here by bills and mouths to feed.
    And even though my day has gone awry
    A five o'clock solution's all I need.
    That timeclock revolution comes and suddenly I'm free...
    Let's fake some memories. Let's go somewhere that no one's seen,
    Where we'll still have never been when we get home.
    Let's fake some memories, Step into a different scene,
    Somewhere we could never get to all alone.
    So close your eyes and don't think twice
    Just grab your books and grab your dice, Let's fake some
memories.
    Sitting here surrounded by my friends,
    Feeling part of something more than real.
    Stepping into someone else's skin
    In tales of magic spells and flashing steel

Where legends come to life and where new worlds will be revealed...

Let's fake some memories. Let's go somewhere that no one's seen,

Where we'll still have never been when we get home.

Let's fake some memories, Step into a different scene,

Somewhere we could never get to all alone.

So close your eyes and don't think twice

Just grab your books and grab your dice, Let's fake some memories.

Defying explanation, more than hype or exclamation,

It's inspired collaboration through a game we love to play.

So much more than fighting dragons, all these worlds that we imagine

All these things that never happened feel as real as yesterday...

Let's fake some memories.

Let's fake some memories, Let's go somewhere that no one's seen

Where we'll still have never been when we get home

Let's fake some memories, Step into a different scene

Somewhere we could never get to all alone.

So close your eyes and don't think twice

Just grab your books, let's roll some dice, Let's fake some memories.

30

LET'S FAKE SOME MEMORIES

In January of 2012, I'd started a gaming group with friends on Monday nights. In the group were Sean, Ty and Randy (who helped make the *Beer Powered Time Machine* podcast everything it came to be) and Ty's young son, William. William was in his early teens, younger then than my youngest is now, but fit in with the gaming group very well.

Not that it matters, but the game system was Savage Worlds, and the setting was a home-brewed version of Steven R. Boyett's novel *Ariel: A Book of the Change*, in which one day technology just stopped working, magic and magical creatures became real, and 99.9% of the population disappeared without trace or explanation off the face of the earth. The game (and the book) were set a few years after the change, with the primary difference being that in the book, the change occurred in the early 1980s, and in our game, the change occurred in 2012. It was a great time, and was William and Randy's introduction to role-playing games. I'm pretty certain Ty had played tabletop roleplaying games before, though they were more often centered on science fiction, *Star Trek* and the like. Sean and I had been gaming together, off and on, since the early 90s, and both of us had been gaming long before we'd met each other.

In any case, the game came to an end, as games usually do, and we moved on to other things, and William grew up and went to college and moved overseas for continuing education and then, well... stayed. Because, like young people do, he'd begun making a life for himself where he was—a life of his own.

So, I was thrilled one day to receive a random message from him thanking me for introducing him to RPGs and letting me know he was running games for his own gaming group. I love the hobby, even more so when I help someone else fall in love with it, and I would've enjoyed gaming with him again, but he was, alas, overseas.

He came home to visit in April of 2021, and while home, he gathered a group of us old gamers together, Randy, Ty, and myself, as well as a friend of ours named Aaron. Not a one of us was under 40 years old, and William ran a game of D&D for us. First, it was wonderful because I don't often get the chance to play, I usually take the role of DM, and that's in large part by choice, but second... He's just a fun, fantastic DM in his own right. He's descriptive and theatrical, fair, and willing to go with the rule of cool, but also able to say no in ways that don't make you feel like he's against you. And even though it was supposed to be a one-shot, we ran very long and ended up finishing the adventure on the second night of the game.

We didn't outright succeed in all the challenges, us crusty, old, experienced gamers—we accomplished our main goal, but unleashed a demon by accident in the process. Three out of four of our characters died in the final encounter. Only one player survived, and that's because the demon decided it wasn't worthwhile to finish us off as we were making (or failing) death saves.It was a great game.

Moreover, it reminded me that there's a continuity to life, and that while I was only trying to enjoy myself and entertain my friends back in 2012, it had affected each of them in different ways. In William's case, it kindled an interest in the hobby that still burned a decade later. It was a very cool experience, and I hope I get to game with him again, in whatever capacity comes along.

It made me think of gaming stories, the false histories of our lives, the vacations that never took place but feel just as real as any heartbreak or success in our real-world lives. At conventions, some folks ask me about my favorite characters and favorite games I've played. I tend to shy away from that, because nobody wants to hear our gaming stories, right? Except that's exactly what this song, "Let's Fake Some Memories" is about. Sit back and get comfortable, because the gaming stories? They're a'coming.

I remember being ten years old, playing at my friend Dave's house over Spring Break, and my character had saved enough gold pieces to purchase a +3, diamond-bladed, lightning sword. It could turn into a lightning blade three times per day and shoot one lightning bolt per day. We fought Slaadi lords in a dark and evil undercity. Dave's mom, Karen, was playing with us as a halfling thief who joined the party mid-adventure a few weeks before. To work her in, my brother (the DM) had her inside the belly of a minotaur we fought and killed. Our killing stroke opened his torso, and she tumbled out, wineskin in one hand, crossbow in the other. If you wanted to drink with her character, fine, but if not, you'd best leave her be. Ten-year-old me got real-world bit on the face by a dog that night. It was bad enough it required many stitches and facial reconstructive surgery. My real regret of the night? It somehow ended the campaign. Never got to play that character or use that sword again.

In high school, I ran a game of Palladium Fantasy Roleplay, and there were between seven and nine players, other than myself. I'd begun giving out experience point bonuses for role playing, so when the not-so-bright fighter, Titus, wanted proof that a sword he was considering purchasing was unbreakable, he swung it against a rack of very expensive swords. I had him roll for the attack. He rolled a natural 20, and I ruled that the swords broke. He argued about paying for the rack of swords, and finally agreed that the shopkeeper would be allowed to take one swing at him with the unbreakable sword in recompense. His character was, as I said, not that bright, but gained a ton of additional experience points for playing in character. Unfortunately, I also rolled a natural 20, and the damage killed Titus. Town guards were abundant, so his ever-present brother and sister couldn't exact open revenge, nor could they afford to pay for a resurrection.

His sister was, however, a warlock, having just acquired a "Create Zombie" spell. She turned her brother into a zombie and they embarked on a quest to have him resurrected, him gaining extra experience the entire way for playing a mindless zombie. It was a fantastic adventure.

Another time in high school, I sat down at the table when my other friends were gaming. They wanted me to play as well, but I told them I'd just watch. One of their characters acquired an intelligent, sentient magical sword within a few moments of me sitting down, and then the group took a bathroom break. I asked the DM if I could play the sword, and he thought it was a fun idea, and I further suggested the sword have two personalities that hated each other, and two different sets of magic powers, and that whenever someone rolled a natural 1 or natural 20, I'd switch personalities. He agreed, and we told no one that I'd be playing. I communicated with the DM via notes, which he then passed to the player holding the sword. That player soon figured out that I was already playing in the game, but the rest of the group didn't catch on until after the session was over. They laughed, because they'd been feeling guilty that I hadn't had a chance to join the game yet, and had been complaining that I should just hop in.

A few years ago, I ran a game in which the main characters (played by our youngest, Jack, our friend Gwen, Sean Smith, and Scott Lindell) found themselves in the middle of an imminent human invasion of the island homeland kingdom of the gnomes. Their characters had discovered early in the campaign arc that the ancient gnomes possessed a weapon known as the Flare Hammer and had a rough idea of where it was. Knowing time was short and that the humans could be arriving any moment, they convinced a member of a secret society to show them the entrance to the hidden sanctuary where the weapon had been locked away. The characters fought their way through traps and puzzles, at length reaching the location of the Flare Hammer. They stepped into crystal chambers to operate the weapon and found that it was controlled by a very limited intelligence that allowed them to see the island and surrounding ocean. It could follow very simple orders, and basically could kill all the people in a certain area, as defined by the users, or anyone of a specific race within that area, up to and including the entire world. They debated how to use the weapon, and as they continued debating, I kept giving them updates describing the landing of the humans' ships, the fighting on the way to the inner keep, the absolute slaughter within the city. The pressure was on and tempers flared.

At one point Sean even suggested killing everyone on the planet. After much debate, they settled on selecting the area surrounding the island and the invading navy, and having the Flare Hammer kill every human in that area. I described the blinding light and the instant disintegration of every human, the slow bewilderment on the bloodied gnomes faces, and the mournful wailing as they tended to their dead and wounded. The players stepped out of the crystal chambers, all but one. The human cleric/rogue was a pile of ashes. The table was full of numb silence. That character's player, Gwen, was moving away, and this was her last session with us. I'd asked her earlier in the week if she wanted her character to die in some dramatic way, and she'd told me that she did, but she'd been swept up in the story, caught in the heat of the moment, and forgotten. Several of us misted up. We took a couple of weeks off from gaming after that night.

These are just a few of the many gaming stories I could tell. I could talk about my brother putting up a flyer in a local grocery store and starting a gaming group made of kids we didn't know in the 80s, which led to me playing an RPG with a girl for the first time. I could tell silly stories of made-up monsters, of cows with cherries for eyes that exploded when hit, or lascivious ogres that turned up when you angered the DM. I could talk about magic items and treasures, about Decks of Many Things and inventive uses for portable holes, and I'm sure many of you could as well, because these absolutely non-existent things were very real to us.

I have a deep and abiding love for roleplaying games and the people who play them. Knowing someone else is a gamer tends to create an instant bond with me. And if you are looking for any real advice about life, love, or anything else, the best I can offer is this: Love the things you love. Share them and proselytize them and don't be a dick and maybe you'll change the direction of someone's life (even if just a tiny bit) and hopefully for the better.

And try not to be George, either in games or life in general, but forgive yourself (and others) when it happens, because it does happen sometimes, and we should look out for each other.

AFTERWORD - THE NOSTALGIA PARALLAX

It was a random, ordinary Thursday night. Well... It was the small hours of Friday morning. I woke up and had to pee, noting that it was after one in the morning. Not a big deal. I'm getting older. I have diabetes. I get up to pee sometimes in the middle of the night. Except... I couldn't go back to sleep. Something happened while I was awake, and I don't know what triggered it, but I started thinking about my past. Events from twenty to as many as forty years ago. I couldn't stop them, and I couldn't go back to sleep.

I was experiencing what I call the Nostalgia Parallax.

On the off chance you don't know what parallax is off the top of your head, it's basically the way something looks different when viewed from two different angles, and it's a perfect fit for what was going on in my head. See... I was falling into what ifs and random thought threads about things that I'm secretly (or really not-so-secretly) ashamed of or unhappy about in my past, These aren't even huge things, not even always specific events, but tiny memories that are so personal and so intimate that sometimes I haven't even shared them with anyone, ever. You know the type.

We all have memories like that, from things that happened while no one's around to things we thought but never said while something else was going on. I started thinking about what I might have done different had I all the information available to me now. I'd hit the Nostalgia Parallax.

I'm not using nostalgia as a good term, here, nor even a bad one. In the 18th century, nostalgia wasn't thought of as an emotion, but a mental illness (one with a very particular meaning, where someone was longing for a specific person or place or object from their past to the point where it affected their everyday lives). I'm using it as more of a neutral term, talking about dwelling on the past, not just a flash of longing for it. Temporarily fixed on it. Maybe a tiny episode of that mental illness from the 18th century.

When I talk about the Nostalgia Parallax, it applies in many ways. Looking back, most of us can see the good and the bad of the past, even things that we didn't know or notice back then. If you're remembering it as idyllic, you're probably overlooking something. Same as if you're remembering it as hellish. Almost always, there was something, or even many things, even if they were small, that were points of happiness during those times.

I'm also talking about the way we perceived ourselves and the world back then compared to the way we see ourselves and the world now, and the way our present self perceives our past selves—and judges them, usually pretty harshly. I spend a lot of time in the middle of the night dwelling on the very poor trailer park kid with questionable hygiene who was always caught up in the little fantasies that I was caught up in back then, and judging that kid through the eyes of an adult who is torn between feeling at home in trailer parks and who also somehow dreads the thought of ever having to live in one again.

And then, also, when we start on the "how we would change things" bandwagon, the different ways we would do things, the different paths we would take if we knew then what we know now, and then we start weighing and measuring every aspect of our lives and comparing them to each other and it gets overwhelming. It gets paralyzing.

And that's why I couldn't sleep. But I know this: if I could go back, I don't think I'd want to. I'd be too tempted to try and change something back then that would affect my life in the same way as stepping on a butterfly in Ray Bradbury's "A Sound of Thunder." Read it if you haven't. If I changed anything, any one tiny thing, what would it mean I'd be giving up now without knowing it?

I like what I have and, for the most part, who I am. I like the changes I've been working on, and the people in my life, and the me I am becoming. And of *course* I was different back thing—everything was different back then. And sure, I'm not the rock superstar or amazing, award-winning actor or director I dreamed of being, nor am I fabulously wealthy. But, like John Lennon sang, "Life is what happens while you're busy making other plans."

Memories are important. They make us who we are, they shape who we become. Still, I need to give the Nostalgia Parallax a rest, I need to give that kid in the trailer park a break. That arrogant, head-strong college kid? I need to give him a break. That balding, middle-aged guy who felt like he was destroying his life and the lives of everyone he touched, as well—I need to give him a break. I need to forgive them all, if I'm ever really going to be happy with who I am, and if I'm really going to get some sleep.

I did get back to sleep, by the way. Last time I looked at the clock was 2:40am, and I focused on fictional characters and a silly fictional storyline to get out of that headspace. It worked, though I was, as usual, still up that morning before the alarm went off. Tricks will work now and then, when they have to, but genuine peace is what I'm working towards, what I hope to find. What I hope we'll all find.

Writing a book like this gave me a reason to reflect back on many times in my life that I might not otherwise have done without doing so through the lens of harsh judgement. Thank you for reading this, for sharing in these scattered memories, for adding an air of borrowed legitimacy to the last two decades or so of my professional life. I'm going to go back to work now, get back to creating songs and stories and memories, but I'll be back.

Until then, be good to everyone. That includes being good to your-self. You deserve it.

ACKNOWLEDGEMENTS

There are so many songs and stories I didn't include, so many people that I didn't mention who deserved to be included. Thankfully, this isn't a proper memoir, or meant in any way to be a complete history of my life. You're welcome for that, by the way. I hope I didn't hurt anyone by omission (or through inclusion, for that matter.)

This book (and most of the the stories therein) was made possible by the unwavering support of my partner in life, Jody, and my children Ben and Laph. I love you all more than words can express, so I won't try. Just know that I understand how very little I've deserved you all having my back in this crazy career of mine. I'm lucky to get to spend my life with you.

Thank you to my publisher and editor, John, for holding my hand through this process and for asking me to do it in the first place.

Thank you to my big brother, Neal, without whom I would never have experienced that life-changing summer in 1983 with red box Dungeons & Dragons.

And finally, thank you to that annoying, needy trailer park kid I was growing up. I wouldn't be who I am if I hadn't been you first. I love you, kid, and I'm sorry for all the times I failed you. I'll try to do better.

ABOUT THE AUTHOR

Mikey Mason spent more than a decade as a full-time standup comedian. He's headlined on all four coasts, performed multiple times each on NBC, at the legendary House of Blues, and the Hard Rock Casino. He even headlined the Atlantis Resort and Casino in the Bahamas, but it wasn't enough.

In 2011, he released a song expressing his geekier side (She Don't Like Firefly) which went viral on YouTube and got him featured on Nerdist online, SyFy, MTV Geek News, The Funny Music Project, DrDemento.com, and even Time magazine. Many albums and hundreds of songs later, his lifelong love for fantasy, science fiction, cats, video- and role-playing games continues to inspire his music and help him evolve, not only personally, but uj7musically and professionally.

Today his profession is creating art and music with geeky themes. His performances are fueled by his passions and sharpened by long years of experience as a stand-up comedian. He's performed at theaters, bars, comedy clubs, casinos, colleges, festivals, and conventions across the US, hosted podcasts, exhibited at art shows, created a coloring book, and more, continually expanding his horizons as to what his next project will be.

His book, *Confessions of a Geek Bard*, is being released in June 2023 through Falstaff Books.

Learn more at mikeymason.com.

FRIENDS OF FALSTAFF

www.ingramcontent.com/pod-product-compliance
Lightning Source LLC
Chambersburg PA
CBHW020135120726
47903CB00007B/2272